D0279791
894.3

WHEN THE EDELWEISS FLOWERS FLOURISH

BEGENAS SARTOV

Cover by Ibraimov R., 2009
Once upon a time in Asia

HERTFORDSHIRE PRESS

First published in 2012
by Hertfordshire Press
Suite 125, 43 Bedford Street
Covent Garden, WC2R 9HA, United Kingdom

© 2012 Begenas Sartov

Printed in Turkey by IMAK OFSET

All rights received. No part of this book may be reprinted or reproduced or utilised in any form or by any electronic, mechanical, or other means, now known or hereafter invented, including photocopying and recording, or in any information storage or retrieval system, without permission in writing from the publishers.

British Library Catalogue in Publication Data
A catalogue record for this book is available from the British Library

Library of Congress in Publication Data
A catalogue record for this book has been requested

ISBN 978-0-9557549-5-1

978-0-9557549-5-1

CONTENT

WHEN THE EDELWEISS FLOWERS FLOURISH

Preface Notes 2

Chapter 1
The Beginning..5

Chapter 2
Story of Melis 26

Chapter 3
Story of My Father..54

Chapter 4
Story of Alien..92

Chapter 5
The Author's Story..102

Chapter 6
The Gorge where the Edelweiss Flourishes...112

Short stories:

THE ROBOT'S BIRTH 122

PARADOX..128

EXPERIMENT 134

SYSTEM THIRTEEN 140

WITNESS OF THE MIRACLES 146

HUMAN OR ANDROID 152

PREFACE NOTES

Written in the Soviet period and critical of that system people who run and abuse, although acceptance of communism being the way to run a society

Written around Kyrgyz way of life – particularly sheepherding which is main/most important agriculture

Written around Soviet Kyrgyz way of life

Written about relationship Kyrgyz have with their landscape – particularly their high mountains and lakes

Written around some of their long held beliefs about goodness of herbs and plants to cure illnesses

Generation of far sighted ideas – was late 60's early 70's when he wrote.

Demonstrates his great love of poetry and song – arts loved by the whole Kyrgyz nation.

BEGENAS SARTOV: 1945 to 1978

Begenas Sartov was born on 15 August 1945 in Checherin Village in Kyrgyzstan. Though he was only 33 when he passed away he left rich and beautiful works including the first science fiction books written in Kyrgyz, including *The secret of the dark mountains (Kyn Tiibes Toolordun Syry)* and *When the Edelweiss flowers flourish (Mamyry Kyldogon maalda)* as well as poems such as *Open space (Maanai)*.

In his early teenage years he used to help his father herd sheep in the Tian Shan Mountains, and at school he published the school newspaper which included his short stories, satires and poems. In 1962-63, when Begenas was still helping his father with herding and farming he wrote poems such as *Moon Traveller (Aiga Sayakat)* and *Spaceman (Cosmonavt)*. These were published in two Kyrgyzstan-wide newspapers, *Kyrgyzstan Pionery* and *Leninchil Jash*.

In 1963, Begenas went to the capital Frunze (now Bishkek) to study at Kyrgyz University of Philology. In 1966 he married Altynkyl Sartova, and they went on to have two boys and two girls, and subsequently ten grandchildren. After graduating in 1971, Beganas went on to work as an assistant filmmaker in the Kyrgyz Film Studio. From then until his untimely death he worked his way through the ranks of two Kyrgyz publications *Kyrgyzstan* and *Meken*, finally becoming Chief Editor of both.

From the late 1960s Begenas was a leader of the *Too Jyldyzy Group*, where he inspired and assisted young and talented Kyrgyz writers many of whom subsequently became well-known in the country.

As one of the Soviet Union's leading science fiction writers, in 1976 Begenas was invited to attend the second world gathering of cosmonauts in Moscow where he met Cosmonaut Grechko – the second Soviet Cosmonaut to travel into outer space after Yuri Gagarin.

When the Edelweiss flowers flourish.

Although writing in the science fiction genre, Begenas often portrayed his own life experiences, as well as the contemporary political and social climate, often exploiting the uneasy relationship between Soviet technological progress and the traditional knowledge of the Kyrgyz in his narrative. In his work When the Edelweiss Flowers Flourish, the leading character Melis is torn between the two worlds. His given name, Melis, derives from the surnames Marx, Engels, Lenin and Stalin. The narrative reveals how the alien Silem (the anticopy of Melis who is given his name in reverse) travels to earth in order to obtain edelweisss plants to help save his own planet from a deadly virus. However the alien finds that he cannot actually strip the planet of this plant as that would be theft and violate his own planet's laws.

The essence of this story was attributed by Begenas to his experience as a child when an old village man helped him recuperate after he broke his arm, successfully using a herbal mixture of seven grasses. These grasses – Edelweiss, Ermen, Ak kadol, Shyraajyn, Oo koroshyn, Kokomirin and Shybak – are still found in the high Kyrgyz mountains today, and are still widely used for their medicinal properties.

At the end of the book, one of the main characters says:

"I am going to [develop a cure for cancer] using only herbs and natural products. But I am going to do it in a studious and scientific manner with proper experimentation, so I can educate others in the field!"

In his work, Begenas found ways to implicitly criticise what he saw as the imperfections of the USSR. Yet at the same time he readily accepts the Communist system as a way of running a country. His writing often reflects the harsh realities of Soviet life: from repression, the black economy, censorship and lack of democracy to faking of scientific research, hollow slogans, and hidden agendas. Meanwhile, he advocates for a different lifestyle that would encourage conservation and careful treatment of the planet, seemingly drawing on his interest in Shamanism, and reverence for the nomadic traditional lifestyle of the Kyrgyz people. The theme of rebirth is repeated often in his books and short stories which may well have been him questioning the Soviet atheistic belief.

In the context of a shepherds son, in what must be regarded as one of the less developed areas of the Soviet Union and at a moment in time (1960's and early 1970's) when his access to happenings in the world and other science fiction literature would have been very limited it is remarkable how his imagination led to stories that are still relevant today. Many of his ideas were very far sighted and original for that time and with such limitations on information within the USSR it can only have been a highly active, intelligent and inquisitive mind that gave rise to his work.

Begenas died young and well before his time. In the final chapter *When the Edelweiss Flowers Flourish*, his last work, he writes his own epitaph:

There used to be fire in me
But this feeling will be gone soon
I will never see you in my dreams
I will sleep forever.

I will never see you in my dreams…
Flowers will bloom on my grave.
Even then I will be faithful to you…
The cloud in the sky
Will cry from time to time.

Chin up and sing a song
Life is beautiful, enjoy it!
I am gone. I leave for you
The pleasure of life….
You know who I am:
I am not going to write my name.

This poem remains carved on his gravestone to this day.

We have endeavoured to translate his work from Kyrgyz to English in a true manner with little embellishment or changes to the subject matter. Equally we have left many of the descriptive phrases as we have found them rather than use more modern language. We hope you enjoy his work.

Shahsanem Murray

Niece to Beganas Sartov

CHAPTER 1
THE BEGINNING

My achievements are great
Life is like a flash of lightning
My life has been spent holding my pen,
But it has been my pleasure
Yes, I am that voice from the future:
back as a miraculous echo

Melis read the letter again and again. Part of it had been underlined three times in pen – "Come over as soon as possible Rena is very ill. She asks about you a lot."

After the last fight they had together, the words almost crushed his heart.

He read on "Maybe her heart would melt a little if you visited. She seems worried and sad: maybe it would make her feel happier, livelier …"

Holding the leather bridle straps in his hands as he rode, he looked up to the high pastures where the sheep were grazing. He took his cigarettes from his breast pocket and pulled one out with his lips. He struck a match and lit the cigarette, shielding it from the wind. After two or three deep pulls he looked at the letter again. Instead of stark blue words he saw graceful smiling lips, acutely intelligent dark green eyes -the cheeky laughter and face of Rena looking back at him.

Melis and Rena had met at the New Talent Literature Festival. The Festival brought together talented youngsters, full of passion with fire in their eyes. They took to the stage and read their own works to the crowd. The established authors of the day always attended, listening attentively to the new works.

Mr. Bolotbekov, the principal member of the Union of Writers glanced at his sheet and introduced the next speaker:

"Rena Shambaeva from the Number 4 Institute of Technology."

The crowd and the members of the Presidium on the stage stared at him their interest aroused: "Who is she?"

From the edge of the audience a girl stood up, her left hand clasping her work book while her right hand flicked a strand of dark hair from her eye. She headed to the stage. Melis, sitting in the second chair in the third row, saw her flushed cheeks and guessed she was nervous.

So yes, that was her he thought: the girl who wrote about "The Sad Mountains" had captured his attention. That was Rena then: more beautiful than he could ever have imagined.

She was indeed beautiful, with a smooth complexion, large green eyes that sparkled like blackberries after the rain, long dark eyelashes and fine hair framing an aristocratic bone structure - a bright being.

But a lack of confidence was sensed by the crowd and some people were whispering to each other. This was the first time Rena was going to recite her poems in public and to her it felt that the crowd knew that – they had found her out. She stood speechless, staring out, feeling hundreds of eyes staring back and sensing whispers of "We'll see how talented she is now". Mr. Bolotbekov caught her eye, gave her a warm and welcoming smile and nodded his head in encouragement. "Now my dear, you may start …" The crowd hushed

This was all the encouragement she needed. She turned her long neck gracefully like a swan to glimpse out of the side windows at the lush greenery, and the confidence flowed back into her like the breeze in the crown of a tree. She turned back to the audience and her recital flowed out.

Melis listened carefully to her poems about the mountains and the clouds. They were full of passion – so much better than those published in magazines and newspapers – they made him feel warm and special. The deep meanings of the lyrics and the protagonist's wonder at the mountains showed him that she knew her subject well.

He thought the words of her last poem ended strangely "…..forgive me, Edelweiss, for my late love."

As she finished she stood still. Once she moved, applause burst from the crowd and continued until she returned to her seat: everyone looked at her with deep respect. She tried to hide her blushing face, staring hard at the back of the man in front of her, unable to bring herself to look at those nearby. Melis looked back over to her but her head was bowed and her face wasn't visible. He wondered if she had ever seen a real Edelweiss flower or if it had all come from books.

The next new "talents" went on stage to recite their work but compared to Rena they were for Melis difficult to understand and only confused him as their meanings blew over him.

"And now we have Mr. Melis Emirov" proclaimed Bolotbekov. After another survey of his script in the extended silence Bolotbekov looked up and surveyed the audience looking for someone to acknowledge the name and come to the stage.

Melis however was deep in thought and had not registered his name being called. "Well, come on now, who is Emirov? Don't be nervous! Stop shaking! Are you with us?" intoned Bolotbekov, looking round the audience and trying to inject some humour the crowd responded with laughter. As Melis reentered reality he rose, and the crowd saw his shiny shaved head: he certainly did not look like any of the other speakers and curious murmurs spread.

"I am a shepherd" stated Melis in explanation as he made for the stage.

"What does that make us?" shouted one of the crowd, and the laughter grew.

"I am also a long-distance horse rider, not just a shepherd," replied Melis good humouredly

The wag retorted "Today is about poems not sheep" and the laughter grew louder again. To Melis it sounded as if the auditorium would burst apart.

"Well let's start to recite some poems then" said Melis, a little confused, as the crowd calmed down
"At last he's realised. Leave the sheep alone!" came the calls from the audience, but the moment had passed and no-one laughed.

"If I did not have my sheep to watch I would not have time to write poems!" continued Melis in his deep voice and at that he started to recite from memory Edelweiss – the Shepherd's poem.

People who live in the mountains call Edelweiss the mountain's soul.
The soul of the mountains is the queen of flowers
She only grows in the highest mountains
Far, far away where only eagles can live
Only those with deep passionate love of the mountains
Can take the flower and dedicate it to their loved ones
But not everywhere can it be found
Because they cannot reach the home of this flower
These flowers which bid farewell to sunsets in the highest peaks
They flourish late because the snow in the mountains melts late
They struggle hard to endure
They survive with passion until time compels them to pass away
The snow arrives early in the mountains
They fight with extremes of weather and flourish like fire
And the life of this flower is like the brightest flame
The soul of the mountains can be reached by a lad
And he can bestow it on his loved one when feelings arise
Feelings of a heart bleeding from love
Brave men who live in the mountains
And who haven't been touched by these tender flowers
They have no right to celebrate love
Soul of the mountains, symbol of the fight, high and blue sky
Flowers of freedom – the symbol of real and strong fighters who will never give up

Melis continued his recitation of the long poem. The audience listened carefully to every word - trying to understand and decipher all the deep meanings.

Mr. Bolotbekov looked concerned and kept glancing at his watch and his papers, but he could never say stop to anyone in the middle of a recitation.

After finishing, Melis returned to his seat to loud praise and applause. Afterwards more talented new people took to the stage to perform their compositions to the crowd. At the end of the programme, famous writers gave practical suggestions to the youngsters on reading and writing literature and the discussions ran for a long time.

"Dear friends! It is already late. We should finish for today but we will all meet again tomorrow at ten. Tomorrow we will break into groups and each section will discuss and debate all the new poems and the findings will be aired tomorrow. What do you think?" enquired Mr Bolotbekov.

With everyone agreeing, the crowd dispersed after visiting the cloakroom. Melis was one of the last to go outside and there he saw Rena, standing in the middle of a group of youngsters. He wanted to join them but wasn't brave enough. "I should meet this girl and have a discussion with her before I leave," he thought. "Wouldn't it be brilliant to be in the same group tomorrow?" Melis didn't know any famous writers or anyone with pretensions of being a great writer. He looked around and then started walking away alone. Around him shouts of "let's go to the restaurant" or "lets head on out to the theatre" rang out, but he didn't hear any of them. All Melis could think of was who the lucky guy would be for whom Rena would shine with her smile. His jealousy grew. He was still wearing his warm boots from the military service of last autumn and he trudged with them through the snow back to the hotel. He pushed on too hard and suddenly slipped and fell to the ground, his hat rolling off. He closed his eyes and thought in his dark world that nobody had seen him, thus saving him from embarrassment. As he tried to get up he realized his legs were sore so he sat and massaged them. At that moment he heard a sound though the frosty snow and started to pull himself together, looking for his hat in the process. Then a voice close to his right ear, like a whispering snake. "It doesn't hurt does it? It's going to be OK, only I saw it, nobody else. Here's your hat."

Melis' sweat trickled down to his eyes: it was Rena

"Thank you" he managed.

He put his hat on straight away, and then took it off again immediately, trying to be polite. As he got up they stood quietly for a moment. He thought she would go now and didn't rush to say anything. Eventually he ventured "I thought you were going to the restaurant with your friends?"

"Which ones?" she replied surveying a group heading off in the distance. "Ah them! They would like to be friends. We talked and they invited me to join them, but I refused."

"You should go" said Melis

"Why?" enquired Rena

"You shouldn't turn down an invitation."

"But I don't know them very well."

"Well, you would after spending time with them!"

Melis was struggling for conversation when she looked up into his eyes. He noticed that he made her a little nervous and smiled as he continued "Please don't worry. I don't know anyone either. That's why I haven't asked anyone out. I did desperately want to talk to one person today ….."

"Who?"

"Well not just anyone actually, but you!" said Melis.

"But we are talking" she smiled.

"I was very keen to meet with you after your poems. I could hardly contain myself …"

"Really! Well let's get acquainted."

Melis stepped towards the girl but his leg was in agony after his slip and fall in the snow and he bit down on his lip.

"Let me help you," she offered noticing that he was limping. And as she helped him, they began to walk and talk easily about everything.

From time to time Melis stopped, but his legs weren't bothering him anymore. Engrossed, he quickly asked her where she came from and learned that she had grown up in the mountains. Her parents had separated and had left her in an orphanage, where she had spent most of her childhood. Now she was in her third year of studies. She then asked him to tell her about himself.

"We are in your city, surely you should be showing me some hospitality first," teased Melis.

"Oh my God, welcome to my city!" said Rena, with a big smile supporting his humour "Yes; it's a Kyrgyz tradition and our culture. Let me take you to see the big city!"

"What's your suggestion?" he asked.

"My residence - Room No.100, Second Student Dormitory?"

"No, no... Not with my country clothing. I'd be embarrassed in front of your sophisticated friends. It would be much better to cook in a big Kazan[1] on a fire right here…"

Rena liked his train of humor and talking and encouraged him "How on earth are we going to get a Kazan my brother?" rolling her eyes.

The young man in him saw her flirting, and felt a tightening at his stomach.

They ended up in the Restaurant "Kyrgyzstan ". It was busy and loud but the waitress eventually found them a quieter corner to sit in. As they looked round they saw the young people from earlier, all seated around the musicians.

"Look, it's your friends," shouted Melis over the noise of the dining area.

"You couldn't find better friends for me" she said sarcastically. "That young chap in the corner, his name is Berdi, his poems are very nice. It looks like a free show is about to start."

"His voice is louder than the others and he loves himself: loudness without meaning?" said Melis, somewhat surprised at his jealousness.

Both of them sat quietly for a while, not sure whether or not to argue, just staring at each other. They were probably beginning to get drunk, and as they both realized this they started to laugh. The waitress arrived, breaking the uncomfortable moment, and they ordered.

As the evening progressed, Melis eventually caught a waitress "Sister, a favour please. Three bottles of champagne for that table, and also take this note to them," he yelled over the din pointing at the 'friends' at the table "and please say it is with great pleasure from us."

The champagne bottles were dressed in Elechek[2] to look like miniature Kyrgyz brides, and as the waitress delivered them to the four young, loud and drunk young men she also passed them Melis' note and pointed over at his table, indicating their benefactor. In turn they read the note and digested the words "Young men. A horse never kicked his owner. Dear friends, we will see you tomorrow. "

Slowly the words sank in and their meaning gradually ended their joviality.

---

[1] Kazan – a very large steel cauldron for cooking food used throughout Central Asia
[2] Elechek - Kyrgyz traditional long white head-dresses, that women wear after marriage

"This came from that stud head," shouted the one called Alybai, as if shouting to the whole restaurant. "Look at his shiny head…. Berdi, I think I will ask him outside so that you can talk to him," and at that he started to slide out of his seat.

"No, no," retorted Berdi and hauled Alybai back to his seat "He only did this to show off to that beautiful girl and make himself feel good. A simple solution is all that is needed!" and at that he caught a waiter and sent two bottles of vodka back to his benefactor!

Barely five minutes had passed when the waitress appeared again in front of the four young men with four bottles of brandy for their table.

The four looked at each other, and in hopeless resignation Berdi summed up all of their thoughts: "Well I doubt we'll be able to top that, so we'll just have to drink it."

And they did!

As the last drops drained from their glasses, and full of alcoholic bluster, Tyko slid out from their table and ambled over to Melis. Between anger and bravado he slurred that he was looking for an apology for the girl and wanted Melis to meet him outside in the toilet for a "quiet word": ironic in itself as half the restaurant heard.

Inside the toilet there were four of them.

"Let's introduce ourselves, hero! My name is Berdi."

"Melis….."

"My Melisium," said Alybai sarcastically. "You are a dope head, not a Melis, a Shiny Shepherd Head! You are just showing off to that girl, eh? You must have lots of money?"

At that the toilet door slowly closed.

"Calm down. Let's talk. I didn't show off. You are writers as well and …I just wanted to meet you."

"What a friendly chap he is" retorted Alybai and the first blow landed on Melis' stomach. Pain passed through him like lightning and then a kick arrived behind his thighs, courtesy of Tyko. From here on things became almost comical. As Melis straightened up from Tyko's kick his head connected with Berdi's chin, sending the latter sprawling. At the same time Alybai let loose a punch, which caught Melis on the cheek and sent him towards the row of cubicle doors. As Alybai fired off a second punch, all Melis had to do was open one of the doors and the punch made perfect contact with it. The door slammed into its frame only to bounce straight back out and catch Alybai right in the face as he followed through his punch. Two down – Melis had been lucky and he duly legged it outside.

Rena was waiting for him, and as she saw his swelling cheek her concern grew "Did you fight?"

He tried to lie "No the door lock got stuck and when I pushed hard it opened, and then sprung back in my face."

"You are lying" she said as she peered at his face: "this is from a fist! Oh Lord!"

"Shhh, please… quiet. They started the fight but I ended up running away."

"Where are they now?"

"Let's get out of here quick."

"There they are…"

"Let's not rush. They tried once and I'd hope they won't try a second time." insisted Melis.

"No, let's get out of here," begged Rena…

"You don't want to eat. I'd like to try their roast chicken!" Melis tried to joke.

"No, I've had enough, more than enough!" insisted Rena again. "Why oh why do such people drink?"

"But we are talented people and we have had a little drink as well!" answered, Melis

"Of course, we have just met each other. I know them a little bit. They are youngsters who really only have their talent and pens, and have only just begun to write. Berdi has published a newspaper – 'Al'manah' – have you read it?" enquired Rena.

"It isn't a great one ...... I really did wish to meet him so many times however I am scared of them for some reason."

"He is like a burning fire for me: an empty void without air that you cannot hold and at the same time a hot living entity. True, isn't it?"

"Well, it sounds like you are in love with him," said Melis, mockingly yet accusingly.

Rena ignored him as she was far away in her own thoughts and continued: "He deserves a big love in his life. Have you read his poem 'Traveler and Lover?' Oh... it could only be written by a man with a great heart. His friends are not good for him – they are a bad influence. If a real writer doesn't drink and doesn't love women he's like ordinary wood, that's their motto. I have one female friend from the University who does know him. She only writes poems about love. That girl always talks well about Berdi. She says he pays a lot of attention to his friends even if they are not there with their pens and are not writing something good. Is that not a sign of a human being? I thought so."

"Well even though he looks wise there are some dark sides as well," said Melis trying to say something positive.

Just then the four of them arrived back in the restaurant somewhat sheepishly. The others, busy arguing over something, didn't even notice.

Tyko was trying to sort out his chair but he stumbled and hit the table with his head. The chair started shaking and knocked the table and some glasses were broken. Everyone in the restaurant turned to see what had happened. A waitress went over and asked them to behave themselves, pay up and leave the restaurant as soon as possible.

Rena and Melis, for some reason, were busy with their own thoughts and noticed little. They quickly finished their dinner, took their two bottles of vodka to the back, and then left the restaurant.

As they walked slowly down the street, they suddenly became aware of an argument on the other side of the road. Melis saw who the four people were and immediately turned into a quieter road.

"Rena," said Melis as he lit a cigarette, "Now they will come and attack me. You stay safe. If they beat me really badly call the emergency number please. OK?"

"I can't let you fight again" and at that she hugged the young man. "They can't attack you while I am with you: they would be too embarrassed."

"They are drunk – they will have forgotten about embarrassment."

"Let's run then…."

"If I was alone I would run, but when I am with a girl running would be like death as it wouldn't take them long to catch up," said Melis.

Suddenly a shout was heard "Hey you, donkey, stay put." And at that the gang of four came upon them. The tallest pushed Rena away, stood in front of Melis and gripped his coat lapels. One of them seriously and painfully held on to Rena until she screamed. At that the others crowded around. Melis shook himself free, and threw his coat to the ground. The fighting started again. It didn't take long as the drunken youngsters were falling unconscious one after one another. Rena pushed her way back in when all had stopped.. When she saw that Melis wasn't injured, she was amazed. She lifted his coat from the snow and put it over his shoulders.

"Hurry, put it on or you could catch a chill," she said as she smiled "you really are a tough one."

Melis was beginning to walk away when he stopped suddenly and turned to look at the bodies lying in the snow "Well yes but they were drunk… They could die here."

"Just leave them alone. I want to get away from this place now."

"What? But what are we going to do about them?"

"They will be sober in a couple of hours and they can get themselves home."

"What if they can't get up and sleep forever?"

"I have never heard of city boys getting so drunk that they froze to death."

"All right, you may be right. But what about our humanity…?"

Rena looked at the young man before her with a big smile on her face "If they were drunk they could accidentally kill you here, and your humanity would not have counted," she nearly said. Because she was so scared and already hated them, she didn't feel sorry for them anymore. "Well, you do what you want and I will follow you like an idiot." She began to shed tears from her big intellectual eyes.

That was her - shy with her feelings and unable to ignore her conscience. Melis felt he was in a deep hole and made a quick decision.

"Do you have a two kopeek coin?" As Rena gave him the coin they made their way back to the payphone near the restaurant. Melis took a notebook from his pocket and called somewhere.

"Hello. Is Kadyr available? Where? He is on night duty. Which room? Do you have the telephone number? It's me, Melis. Don't worry. Tomorrow, Erkettai. I said tomorrow... Tomorrow... Bye"

Melis then called another number.

"Hello is that the police? I need Amantaev. Oh it's you. Why are you mumbling? What? I see: you have just arrived. Yes, thank you. Well, I need a favour. You are on call so bring one more colleague please and come over fast: I'm by the Restaurant "Kyrgyzstan". Sure let's leave it at that just now. Will talk to you later, sure.... Bye"

They returned to the fight scene and started counting the sleeping bodies.

"I thought there were four of them, but there is one missing," said Melis, his voice deepening with the effort. "Maybe he ran away."

"Ah yes, I saw one of them do a runner – probably to the park" said Rena.

"Maybe he is a demon."

Melis collected all their passports and documents from their pockets, so he could return them next day, when they will sober up, and put them in Rena's handbag. It wasn't long before the police car arrived. The two friends greeted each other warmly.

"Kadyr, we were together at the restaurant before we left. These big young guys came and beat us up."

"Yeah, yeah, bullshit. You used to beat people up by yourself. You were the people's Greco-Roman wrestling champion."

"I had to protect this girl: that's why I didn't fight."

Kadyr laughed very loud. "Well, that's just your version of the story."

"They need to sober up quickly. Take them to the special facility to sober up. "I'll come early in the morning and pay all their penalties and bail them out myself. Okay, friend?"

They put all the drunken people to the car.

"Kadyr, please look after them well. I'll visit your house tomorrow. Tell Erkettai she should prepare well for us."

"So long."

"Goodbye."

They took a taxi together and reached Rena's dormitory just after midnight.

They knocked on the door for a while before the concierge showed up.

When she saw Rena she opened the door right away.

"Mrs Elena Ivanova," said Rena in a begging tone "This man is a brother for me. We were late coming back from the cinema; we had to wait so long for a bus. But we just got here now. Please, we will wait till morning if possible."

The old lady didn't believe the story and stared at him for a while then told them "There is a sofa in the lounge. I'll make a cup of tea and you, dear, bring your towel. We need to put his eye on a hot towel. It looks like your brother's eye will be black tomorrow!"

Rena only then noticed that Melis' right eye had been injured, she was so upset.

"I'll fetch it right away," she said, disappearing to quickly return with a towel.

Oh???… Rena was so fragrant, when she attended to him (it was her perfume but it seemed natural). She put her towel in hot tea and put it to his injured eye. It was on that night that their friendship started.

Next morning they went to the police station together to bail out Berdi and the others and Melis returned their passports. They all went to a café, and after the hangovers diminished they set off back to the Institute for the poetry readings.

Little did any of them realize that they would all return as guests to the house of his friend Kadyr, the policemen who had collected them all, many times in the future.

After that episode Berdi, Tyko, Alybai, Rena and Melis all became best friends. They were virtually inseparable until Melis went his own way, passing exams to enter the Agricultural Institute thus leaving the Philology Institute, even though they all tried to convince him to change his mind. The remaining four stuck together, and graduated and celebrated together, while Melis was still frying in the hot sun and taking exams at his University in the hot summer time.

Rena start working in Sokuluk area: as a deputy technologist in the spirit factory, then as a chief technologist until, Rena became a Komsomol secretary for that district: now she's been there for three years. . Berdi started working as an editor in a publishing company. Tyko was jobless for a while but finally found work for a radio station. Alybai was a great teacher until he went into politics and became a deputy.

"Ooh … it's been such a long time, so long yet it's only one year since I got my diploma" thought Melis.

Only Berdi and I are still the same. He is still an editor in a publishing company. And I am still a shepherd in my village.

At some stage Melis smiled with his sour long face, then shook the bridle and judiciously prodded his horse with his heels to get it to move. His horse was normally calm but this time he frightened it a little and it set of at a pace until he reined it in. Everything was happening unexpectedly. He was even in danger of falling off his horse.

His sheep were everywhere, spread around near Kyr Jol. Melis pushed his horse to walk faster and they found a cool place with a gentle fresh breeze. He jumped off his horse and took off the saddle. Then he put a bag of food to the horse's mouth and let his horse, Tory Kashka, eat. He tied the reins around his legs to stop him wandering off.

He spread his little traditional handmade patchwork korpocho, and put his saddle to one side of it so that he could use it to prop his head as he lay down. He pulled out his letter from his chest pocket and read the same thing over and over again.

"….maybe her heart would melt a little if you visited... maybe it would make her feel happier, livelier … Please, we just need you to come over to the city. There's a lot of things to talk about. Will you? Yours sincerely, Berdi"

Over the past two days Melis had already read this nearly sixty times. He couldn't decide, and felt torn.

He remembered last year's events and still couldn't see how he had made any mistakes.

When he graduated from University, all his friends had gathered together. He didn't even ask any of them, they just arrived by themselves. Maybe Berdi had organised it all beforehand.

They went to the Ala Archa Gorge Park where there was a little river surrounded by beautiful blackberries, and looked for a place to stop. Alybai had brought a whole carcass of a sheep. His brother-in-law, who had driven the private car, was cooking for everyone.

Rena and Tyko's private drivers were far away in Kyzyl Shagyn to pick yshkyn[3]. Alybai's wife, who had just given birth, stayed at home because it was a long drive from Issyk Kul to Frunze.

Tyko's wife was in holiday in Talas. Berdi's wife, Joogazyn, was working to her timetable, and was busy that day so couldn't be with them either.

---

[3] Wild leeks found growing all over the hills of Kyrgyzstan in the spring – they have a very sour taste

But there was green grass with lot's food spread on the table-cloth and they were five of them: Five friends!

Alybai opened the champagne with a loud pop and gave everyone a glass. The first speech came to him.

"I would like to drink this champagne for our Melis. I wish him success and all the best for future opportunities. I would like to say three things. First, I congratulate you on your graduation. Second you should become a teacher and give up being a shepherd. Third, please get married. Ha ha ha. Who agrees? Is anyone going to say anything? No, then we are all agreed. Now please drink this for the main toast…"

Everyone drank their champagne then their attention turned to the spread on the table-cloth, tasty food against the backdrop of the green grass of Ala Archa. Only Berdi didn't drink, and put his glass back. Everyone else continued to drink and wished nice things, they were really having fun. Then it was Melis' turn to speak, and he stood up.

Dear friends, who make me feel as if I am touching the sky, a big thank you and lots of appreciation to all of you. If it weren't for you, my dear friends, I might not have been able to graduate from University at all. It's only because of you that I have my diploma. Of course you worried that I couldn't make a decision myself. I thought a lot but I can't change suggestions because in this life everything should happen when the time is right. I cannot be a teacher. My parents are old and I can't leave them alone and move to the city. That's why I should remain a shepherd: that's the right thing to do… My parents have healthy habits that will lead to long lives: in the summer they will go with herds of horses to the high and green Jailoo[4] and drink kymyz[5]. Then I can get married. But who is the bride? When I was graduating from school there was only one girl I used to write to. She told everyone at the school, laughing at me and making me look like an idiot. After that episode I struggle to say the word "Love" to anyone. Well let's drink this toast to the hope that one day I can say "I love you" to a girl."

Everyone stood up and drained their glasses.

As Melis finished and they began to sit, Berdi started his toast almost straightaway.

"Once upon a time, you made us behave correctly, I will never forget that. If we had never met you, we would not have any pride in ourselves. We used to write poems with the wrong themes 'women and drink'. We were foolish then and it looks like we would never have got to where we are today, who knows. Thanks to your

---

[4] Green summer pasture
[5] Fermented horse milk

hard push, look around us. Alybai became a teacher: not bad at all! Tyko became a journalist. Rena is a Komsomol. And I joined the writers union. Well it's all because of your good example."

Berdi continued: "Look back, we all remember all the good things you both wished us after we sobered up and went to your dear friend Kadyr's house. So much good came of it! But this is just your good dream about us, which all came true! It's as if we were your solders: under your command, of course, you are three years older than us, and it worked out perfectly. And maybe it was your own dream that your own life should change in this way? Now I am sure of that."

"We used to be like soldiers and you like our commander – a little older than us and making all these changes. Of course there are no regrets but now in our shadows, you are still the same, and you don't even want to change your own life, for some reason, like a fresh little spring chicken? You could easily already have been author of three or four books. I didn't write my best novel, you always say, and you've never been to a publisher. It's not right." Berdi pulled his handkerchief from his pocket, carefully polished his glasses, and put them back on.

But, it is not too late. You still could reach some good points, if you will even start now. We have a deputy editor position. You should come now, as your parents don't have so many animals to look after. They could just take a few, privately-owned sheep to the Jailoo.

"That's right," said Tyko with a happy smile. "Lots of old people go to the Jailoo by themselves. Don't be scared of getting a job. If you are really keen on working in radio, there are several chief editor positions just waiting for you, and they would totally suit you, just imagine!"

"Melis should just be a teacher in his own village. He is now used to a village life style, aren't you?" said Alybai stating his opinion and clapping Melis on the back. "If you get married, the village will be just great for this."

Rena was staring at Melis with big smile thinking, "Well then make your decision. The time has arrived!" She didn't say anything.

Melis was stuck completely. He started thinking about the "Soul of Mountains" where the edelweiss grows very high. Then he thought about Silem. He should be returning back to Earth in one year.

Silem and his comrades should return to Earth from their planet soon to accomplish their mission. To ensure their expedition has an ethical result, that's why he couldn't give up the mountains or being a shepherd.

He smiled then started again, trying to change the subject. "No, dear friends, I have done some things well after all. I am best maker of meat in our valley. Isn't that enough to be proud of?"

For a while they all encouraged him to give up being a shepherd. As the main dish arrived, Melis was able to hide his own uncertainty as his mind swirled around the subject, but always reached the same conclusion as before: to stand tough and not change his mind.

After holding her tongue all this time, Rena couldn't stop herself anymore.

"Oh, just leave him alone... you will count sheep's feet and stay in the mountains forever. If you do not think about yourself, think about other people too. You are really stubborn and selfish, and have a twisted mind. It's you I am waiting for: when will you say 'I love you' to me? How long do I still have to wait for you? I am getting older now, time is passing me by. Not only my best years are passing, but the best year of my whole life is passing this year – I am 28. Now I am officially an old woman. How much gossip must I listen to, and I was so passionate! Who am I to you? You think I am a deep sea to you, without any feelings or waves. Or I can't find another man like you. How many men used to kiss my every step desiring to marry me? Oh God. Shame on you. Grow up. You are not seventeen either. How long should I wait for a joker like you to bring me the "soul of the mountain". How long should I wait? Enough... That's it. You have only two ways out. Either you give up your sheep and start working or get out of my life forever and follow your stupid sheep. That's it – did you hear me?"

The others went very quiet.

Melis didn't look at Rena, but turned his head down to the two drivers, who were returning with a bunch of yshkyn.

"I didn't know that you loved me so much Rena! I was trying to bring the 'soul of the mountains' to you. You should know that well... All my poems were dedicated to you. It's not because of me having studied till this time. We are supposed to be happy together but there are higher things in this life.

Great things will be achieved in one year. If we make the right decision, then not just you and I but the whole planet and millions of other people will be really happy in the future. That's why: there are higher things in the world than our feelings, and we should even been prepared to sacrifice our lives for them," said Melis, He looked at everyone and pleaded: "Please give me one year."

"Why do you need one more year? If you would like to say something, can't you tell us now" said Alybai disappointedly, whilst all the time inwardly raging and thinking "Because of you, I didn't marry Rena and I've married another woman. If you are not going to marry Rena, I will kill you right away."

"Sure tell us now" said Tyko with drunken anger. He also knew that Melis loved Rena, and that's why he had married a different girl. He sat inwardly thinking that if Rena had showed any desire for only him he wouldn't have been stupid: he would have taken her right away to his house and would have fought for her to the death if needed.

Berdi was very angry as well "Listen, what do you actually want? Why are you acting like a scabby dog," He was boiling inside. He knew that Rena had lived for Melis all these years. "You cannot be this foolish. You haven't married someone else and hidden her from us. No, that is just not possible! If you make Rena unhappy, shame on you and our friendship is going to end.

"You're so strange, or is it that you want me to kidnap you instead?" Rena was joking and the same time she was angry with herself. "Oh I am such a foolish girl," she was very upset." I was very naïve to wait and hope for his humanity, I was like a goat watching the moon, now I missed my time. If he disappoints me today, it would be better for me to die. There is no reason for living…"

"Well I told you I need one year, only one year. If I said so that means I said so.

"Why?"

"Why? You don't have any other questions? All right, I will tell you then. I will wait for Silem, as he is going to come back."

"Who is Silem?" They all asked at the same time

"Silem is my friend from another world who I am helping …"

After a deafening silence the cries of What??? Explain??? Huh?? rang out from his friends, who wondered if they had misheard.

When the shouts died down and after a further silence Melis began "Everything, every piece of space material has its own anti-duplicate. Things have their own anti-things. Even you and I, we all have anti-copies of ourselves – we have to think this way."

"Wait, are you ill, or is something wrong with you" Alybai put his hand to Melis forehead. "But you don't even have a temperature….. Gosh…"

"Take your hand off me!" said Melis grabbing his hand and pushing him away so hard that Alybai nearly fell over. "Don't treat me like an idiot!" Melis was really quiet for a while then he started talking again "Of course I love Rena. My life without her is meaningless. I cannot even explain how much my life would not be worth having… You all remember how Rena and I misunderstood each other. I promised to give her the 'soul of the mountains' a long time ago. Before I give her this flower, I can't even think about marrying, you all should know about that… Do you remember the first holiday, when Rena and Berdi came over to see me on the Jailoo? "

Berdi cut in "That's right, when we were there all three days we had lovely weather and on the fourth day you took us to the black gorge and your sheep were there. You left us and went to Karala-Aska black gorge by yourself, because you weren't sure that we would be able to reach the place. And we waited so long for you that Rena and I just managed to stop the crazy sheep running away. In the afternoon it rained and then started to snow. Rena and I hid the sheep in the shadow of the mountain and you still never showed up. The sun started shining later but you still didn't.

"Yes. Both of you chased all the sheep back home and then you found me nearby in that spring water under that gorge." continued Melis.

"That time you were sweating and moaning with pain?" said Rena. "You were supposed to give me the flower that day but we couldn't catch you. Instead you found yourself a nice warm place to have a nap and forgot all about us. You didn't even come after us, after we came from the city to spend time with you. You left us in the snow and rain. It was so awful and I cried a lot, but even that didn't make you feel ashamed…"

"If you hadn't left me that day maybe we would already be married by now…" said Melis.

"I never will forget that day and how you made me feel so embarrassed." Rena started crying again. "It looks like you had other things on your mind…."

"But I told you that I nearly reached that highest gorge where the 'soul of the mountains' grows. I found some, and dug a whole bucket of them. Suddenly the rain started and then turned to snow. I thought I would present twin flowers. It was so hard to reach that place. I nearly reached the highest one. Rain was falling like never before, and the wind was blowing so badly I was trapped - I couldn't even breathe. Then just as I reached the place, I stood on something and fell from the mountain. Later I do not remember anything. When you found me and woke me I was sleeping near spring water. I was surprised myself, you do remember that. You didn't believe me at that time and instead of resting you were so angry and left me. Berdi was supporting you and you didn't even want to talk to me. My father and mother heard later that that you had been upset and they were so angry with me."

"Then I would have sorted you out right there at the edge of the spring water. I would have beaten you up so badly "said Alybai. "Your poor old parents, they were so happy when they thought they were finally going to have a daughter-in-law and you …"

"And me, after that mystery story, still after two years going over it all again and again in my mind. When Rena left me in a foul mood the world wasn't the same again, everything was empty for me, sad. I was so depressed that I couldn't hide it from you. Even when I was taking exams in the city I was so upset that I couldn't show my face to my friends. Then Alybai became a member of parliament, and Berdi sent a letter to ask us all to go together to congratulate him. That's how we all found each other again, not so long ago, was it? During that time so many strange things happened … "

Melis took one of his cigarettes and, after pausing for a moment to think how to start his story, he slowly began. "For two years after Rena left me I had really strange dreams. When I understand that my dreams may have been what actually happened to me, I took my father with me to look after the sheep so that I could go to that place again……"

CHAPTER 2
STORY OF MELIS

Who am I?
One little crumb of this planet
A droplet in the stream of life,
Light from a fire passing from today to tomorrow,
A green bud citing word(s) of poetry

After herding our sheep into the gully, my father and I rode our horses to the middle of Tosh Bulak. My father had a chanach[6] of kymys strapped to his saddle. I untied it and placed it beside a big stone. We spread a patchwork blanket korpocho on the green grass, and I passed the chanach to my father.

My father took a sip and said "Here, have some yourself", passing it back to me. I took a few thirsty gulps of the kymys, and balanced the chanach inside a large wild leek plant, covering it from the sun with my waistcoat.

"Well, my son," said my father with a long questioning look "You were going to tell me something this morning?"

I started looking further and further towards Karala Aska. Two eagles were flying high and the sun shone brightly. Our horses were enjoying grazing on the green grass and wild leeks. "I had a dream last night…" I didn't know how to continue. My father looked straight at me – I understood he was worried about something. Maybe he was a little surprised, as I had never believed in dreams or anything superstitious before. My father, on the other hand, was a very religious man while I was an atheist, and we used to have many arguments about this. Our arguments could be so fierce that sometimes he even threw me out of the house, yelling that he would stone me. I often had to spend two or three days hiding in the Karala Aska caves. My mother usually found me, soothed me, warmed me up and took me home to make up with my father. She would tackle him angrily saying: "You maintain your religious ways but do not brainwash my son. If he needs God the time will come."

I never liked hearing my father's old songs about things that had to be done. My mother would say, pointing at me: "Never talk back to your father while he is

---

[6] *Flask made from goatskin which helps to keep cool the liquid inside*

being religious, it's not funny. Shame on you if you do not believe it! Why do you deride others' religion and ways of life! You should stop it. Leave older people alone. Live your life the way you want to. Everyone has their own beliefs – you believe in Communism. Who is casting stones at your beliefs? One day there will be Communism all over the world, that is what you and I believe. But when the Soviet period began your father was already over thirty years old and by that time his view of the world and life had already formed, in the way of his fathers."

She would continue "For many years your father had no children and spent his time praying in the Mazaar[7] – it made him totally religious. He heard your first scream at birth when he was already fifty eight. If you want to know, your father and I have only lived for you. ….." She would start crying "And you make your father upset, why?"

After that my father and I stopped arguing about religion and lived our lives in our own ways. Now as I sat here trying to explain to my father my dreams and memories I suspected that he might be happy, thinking that God had finally arrived in my heart. He obviously wanted me to tell him my dreams so that he could explain them.

"Holy God," he prayed loudly and gestured for me to begin.

"I think I may have had a dream last night but... I do not know if it was a dream or maybe something from my past. I feel lost," I said, and looked straight at my father.

"Do you remember the last time Rena and Berdi visited us? I swore to Rena that I would give her the 'soul of the mountains.' But I couldn't, she was upset … And last night I dreamed that I couldn't give the flower to her," I choked, but couldn't show that to my father. I looked away from him, pulled up a wild leek and started chewing on it. When I bent down for it my father wanted to say something with his shining eyes, but he stopped for some reason. I was shaking, and trying to control myself. I got up and walked away to bring the kymys and take a little sip from the flask. When I offered it to my father he shook his head. I returned the kymys to its place. As I looked around at the sheep my father asked me to sit beside him.

"You shouldn't be looking for the 'soul of the mountains' in the high gorges. It would be better to offer some of the flowers that grow here. That would have been more interesting for the girl," he sounded very disappointed, that he hadn't' told him this before.

---

[7] Old graveyards out amongst the fields

My fathers' words were new for me!

"Why? Does the 'soul of the mountain' not grow in other places anymore?" I asked.

"Of course my son… There are many beautiful flowers that do not just grow in high gorges, there are so many that grow on the face of the mountains as well. They have longer stalks and bigger flowers. When they are arranged with lots of others not too many people know the difference. There is another type of 'soul of the mountains' which we call"Boz unach". You could find them easily at the river bend or the nearby old stony graves. But the ones from the high mountains are the real 'soul of the mountains.' They can only be found by the best hunters, not just anyone, and it is these flowers which can be used to treat thousands of illnesses. Only hunters who climb like mountain goats can collect these flowers. You know how to find them my son," he said with a deep breath "Now let's talk about your dreams!"

"My dream: two years ago I had left Berdi and Rena to look after my sheep and I went by myself across to Karala Aska. You know better than me the places where the eagles make their homes, only the mountain goat could reach them. Last year that hunter Ashylraly, who could shoot straight between the eyeballs of both of us if we were fighting like dogs, climbed up with me and we reached the site together. Yes, Ashylraly pulled me all the way up with a strong rope tied around my body, and he showed me the 'soul of the mountains' that grew in the really high gorges. They were growing there very sparsely. When we got there, Ashylraly was very disappointed, as we had gone too early and it was not yet time for the 'soul of the mountains' to flower.

"So I kept climbing the gorge where the 'soul of the mountains' grows. I had my stick and I had metal horseshoes on my feet for grip It was so exhausting, I sweated like a pig but I saw a single flowering 'soul of the mountain' between the two gorges at the top. It was   shining brightly, and gently fluttering in the north wind. Right at the top white and yellow flowers, strong and beautiful, were in bloom. The colours were marvellous. From time to time the colours seemed to change from yellow to a bright white. I didn't think for long, I pulled the flower up straight away with its roots. I started wandering around looking for more, forgetting the time. Then suddenly the weather changed, and I was surrounded by clouds. The rain started, lightly at first but getting heavier by the minute. Summer, like a little child's moods, is very changeable and I thought the storm would be over soon, so I started climbing higher to find more "soul of the mountain".

"It wasn't long before the rain turned to snow, and lightning struck l around me. My body was shaking with cold and fear of the heavy storm. But I didn't give up and I kept climbing higher. Suddenly, I missed a step, and clutching or something to hold onto; I found nothing .I was falling down. My arms wind milled but gravity had taken hold and I fell backwards out into thin air. My eyes were rolling and thoughts raced through my brain as I reached end of the gorge. Then as I concluded my life was about to end, I saw something bright coming out from the mountain towards me. I quickly caught hold of it and felt that I was pulled in. I saw a strange figure standing in front of me. I landed in a heap at his feet and slowly looked up the stranger. He had shiny new rubberlike footwear, a long and wide leathery coat and a hat with four strong corners. As I stood up I examined his face – long and thin, with protruding eyeballs laced with red veins. He had a travel bag on his shoulder, and in his hand was a pole that resembled a tapered walking stick (I was later to learn that he called it an Asa Musa[8])

Yes, we used to see lots of strangers with that kind of Asa Musa. If he had been riding a donkey, I would have thought that he was a real wandering salesman – the kind who often travelled from village to village selling potions. I stood there staring and, before I could gather my thoughts, he started talking to me in a melodic way.

"Oh don't be amazed young man
This is our destiny
In strange circumstances
We meet each other…"

"I was so scared at that moment. I thought about you, father. You used to tell me that in your religion when a man is in a very difficult situation, he is meant to meet his Maker. I thought that this was such a moment: inside I was praying for God.

"However, as I stared at the stranger it appeared he was laughing and he continued, almost singing his words:

"Oh poor creature of God
You have lived a very happy life
Yet you are foolish
One who thinks that strange things must be magic!"

"He was talking to me in a very amusing way. That's why I couldn't remember everything he told me, so after our conversation I had to think and almost translate it into ordinary words."

---

[8] *A walking stick made from a shrub - Asa- Abelias - native to Asia. It has a special quality of not getting dry or rotten. It is often used as a special "magic stick" by dervishes and beggars because of its unique properties.*

At this point in my story, my father looked worried and started praying. He then stood up and went and washed himself in the stream, put his coat on and then prayed even more. Finally he came back and sat on his knees to listen further.

So I continued my story "The stranger said "Why did you pluck the "soul of the mountain" out by its roots? Who gave you the right to do that? Couldn't you have just plucked the flower itself? That root cannot now grow back even after thousands of years. Did you not know that one flower could help lots of ill beings to get better? Think about it. You have harmed so many people."

"Father, I was angry with him. This stranger, who looked very ill, was trying to say something very clever to me. I actually forgot he had saved my life. I started questioning him "Why are you singing to me, brainwashing me? If you want to say something, just say it!" I was cold and shaking, and my teeth were rattling.

"Look at yourself" I continued "you're so thin it looks like you haven't eaten anything for years. What's your problem? It's up to me if I pull out the roots or just the flowers of the "soul of the mountains". What is it to you anyway?"

"The stranger didn't even react to my anger and coldness. He was acting as if we were together at a big table sharing tea together.

"It is my business as to why I am here in these dangerous gorges. The "soul of the mountain" helps people recover from very bad illnesses - 1000-7-(3)-1. It is the key for a drug against this illness. Now give me that flower. You don't even know what to do with it. "

"The stranger was getting annoyed and made a noise with his stick, shaking it, and then plunged it into the earth. My hand opened and the flower left my hand and levitated over to him smoothly, landing in his open hand. He pulled his stick out from the earth and waved it – a wind blew up, encircling the flower and sucking in snow from all around it until it was totally covered. Then, with another flick of his stick, the wind stopped and all fell quiet. He then produced from his pocket a square piece of what looked like glass and put it to the top of the snow now covering the flower, and he pushed a little button. There was a noise, and the stranger let the square glass float away from him, as it slowly enveloped the snow. When I looked at the snow very closely the glass and the snow had taken on the same shape. Through the glass only the stalks of the flowers were visible.

"You are taking my flower in that thing?" I said to the stranger as I struggled for words.

"Yes, the flower is now well preserved; it will be fine until it reaches my homeland."

"Where is your homeland? Who do you think you are? Where are you from?"

"I come from other side of the planet Earth, six levels beneath, and seven levels above the space, where they meet."

"So, you like joking, do you?"

"It is not a joke. How can I explain it to you? You know about stars and outer space?"

"I started telling him the things I knew, but the stranger got tired and stopped me.

"Everything you told me is only about the outer space that you could usually reach with your way of thinking. It's only a part of outer space - the only part your mind accepts. Imagine a button with thirteen points; use your imagination to think about that button. It's not flat as you think. It has thirteen corners, yet it is round. Only one corner is the part of the galaxy that you usually reach. If you think of the galaxy as the whole button, for you to understand clearly, you will see that all parts of the galaxy are close to each other. There are thirteen levels – and you live in one of them. There are six levels above and six levels below. The galaxies all go round – you can travel from one to another a long way or a short way, it's the same principle. And then the thirteen galaxies together make one mega galaxy. This is the only side of space you can reach with your mind. And the space matter always has its own anti-matter. All matter has anti-matter. For example you have your own anti-copy. That's why thirteen anti-galaxies make a huge anti-mega-galaxy. At the same time anti-anti-mega galaxies exist and they have anti-anti-anti-mega-galaxies. In short, space is unlimited. And it continues the same way."

"I had lost the plot, and had no idea what this crazy man was talking about. I started to think about my flower – what was I supposed to do? I had to get it back. After all, Rena was waiting for me!"

"Stop your crazy story – you have lost me completely. Give my flower back to me!" I said trying to be forceful. "I need to give it to my girl. I swore I would. I found it, so why should you take it from me? There are plenty in that gorge. Go and find one yourself and go back where you belong. Anyhow, who gave you the right to steal if you really do come from another planet? It's very interesting that you come and want to own it. Do you understand? I'm getting angry now: give me back my flower and go back to your " corner thirteen". You can use that wild imagination of yours to invent a better (anti-)planet to belong to and find some mountains of your own."

"We don't have this flower…" the stranger's voice had become more normal and tailed off.

"And what do you think," it struck me that that even I was abusing my right. "When you have picked all the flowers, what are we supposed to do? You said that the flowers are very good for some mysterious illnesses – if one of us is ill then we may need them too! What then?"

"You don't have to worry about that. We are humanoids too – it is in our ethics to look after other planets. We only pick this type of flower once every two years and the last time we only picked three of them!"

"I don't care! You are stealing from our planet. If you pick flowers for medicine from every planet in every galaxy how many planets will you have stolen from?"

"You are the preferred world for us. We can't go to other galaxies and mega-galaxies as they are surrounded by black holes. If you go anywhere near you disappear, never to be seen again even if you are alive within the black hole. Because of these black holes we couldn't maintain our existence and any material that we were transporting would be lost. This is the only anti-world we can visit.

"But you are stealing these flowers from our planet; our part of space!"

"No, we are just collecting them. This rich resource will never be exhausted on this planet. This is the truth. If it ever did disappear the main components of your world that you need could be collected from eight levels under sky and five levels above the sky. In space it is not far away.

"Oh really! Just now you are stealing from our planet and in the future you will be pushing us to steal from somewhere else? Now give me back my flower. I can't let my flower go to a thief like you"

The stranger looked like at me as if I had hit him, as though he were confused by my ruthlessness and misbehaviour. If I gave up, what would become of my flower? "Please you have to understand me" he was now almost begging me "This year we were to collect just this specific flower, the very one which you pulled out by its roots. Eleven years ago during an eclipse the shadow hit this exact point where this flower grew. This particular flower has the properties we need. The others will reach their usefulness at a later time. In this gorge we picked five useful flowers eight years ago. This year there is only one useful flower. And in two years' time there will be four ready on the other side. And way beyond over there just three will be ready in eight years. We do not pick every flower!"

"But you do not ask permission, I don't care what you use it for. You thought you could mess me up with your song. If your mission is so honourable, why don't you reveal yourselves openly? You could develop high-level ties, create diplomatic relations and make ordinary friendship with us. After that whether you could take it or not may not be up to you?"

"You know," said the stranger. "You are not ready for friendly relations. You don't have a unified idea yet. This little planet has so many different countries. One says it wants to have peace and another says it is ready to go to war! You have atomic bombs, neutron bombs and hundreds of other weapons of mass destruction! You mistrust each other and spy on each other. If you used all this power for research instead of to destroy things, it would be priceless. You should have positive cooperative research programmes, to learn about the stars and planets. Then you could use this to develop science and technology to the highest level - to discover the secrets of black holes, find how to fly to anti-worlds and learn about them. We've started researching everything, but we are still not developed enough to find out about this, but we believe we'll be able do it eventually. But to reach this level we stopped thinking about war long ago. Thousands of years ago our planet became one country. We accepted long ago that human beings wouldn't stop fighting each other, and so other planets are not going to have any relationship with them."

"Of course, with your highly developed clever minds and your ethical laws, you have the right to steal."

"It is not stealing. We have no other choice: it's as simple as that. You do not even know how important this flower is; you do not even care about it. You do not use them right now," The stranger then asked, "when the time comes, will you also have ethical laws like us?"

"We are not going to follow your way. We have ours which is good enough for us. If it turns out not to be, we will develop our own rules."

The stranger was amazed and stood looking at me. I didn't care anymore about his sickness. He looked just awful and yet all he wanted to do was talk about some stupid thirteen corners of world and anti-world, and his philosophies. He looked as if he had once been an ordinary physicist. And it looked like he had chilled his nervous system and in the end gone mad to the point where he now dressed crazily. He believed that he came from an anti-world, and was travelling around our world, poor crazy guy... And just to have my flower, he had made up this entire story and was brainwashing me with total bullshit.

""No," I said to the stranger "I can't give away flowers just like that, like some sort of charity. This flower belongs to the person looking after my sheep down there." As I was thinking what to say next the stranger pulled his Asa Musa higher. I thought he wanted to hit me and I started searching for some stones just in case I had to attack him first. Suddenly the fog around us disappeared and everything was clear. It was then that I saw something flying in the gorge beside us. I was so scared but when I looked at it all I could think of was a flying saucer. As I stared it seemed it was indeed a flying saucer, and my brain gradually accepted that it was, and that it was landing on a flatter part of the mountainside about a hundred metres away.

Of course like every educated person in the second half of the twentieth century I had heard stories about flying saucers but I had never believed in them.

"We used to read stories from Italian and German magazines about UFO's. American astronauts had landed on the moon and some flying saucers followed them back to earth. There was a picture, the only one I had seen. For me this was just a science fiction story – flying saucers were stories only. However, two more of the strangers appeared from the flying saucer. They held their Asa Musas at a slight angle, and it seemed that these "sticks" helped them fly closer to us. In just a couple of minutes they reached us.

""Silem, why are you conversing with this stupid thing? Have you preserved the flower? It is time to go. Our leader doesn't understand why we are late. He is angry with us. If we don't reach super orbit-space and enter trans-rocket orbit today then we won't be able to reach it at all. We may have to stay here another year. And you know what that would mean."

"The one I took to be the youngest, and who had been quiet so far, now looked at the second new stranger and quizzically asked "The rocket would stay in artificial orbit and we would be stuck for a whole year in hibernation, like other biological systems sleeping."

""Well this should not be happening. We should go back to our families and retain our right to have another mission," one of them said forcefully. Of the two who had just arrived the younger looked really straightforward, while the older was standing quietly and staring at me.

"But at this moment my stranger tried to stop him.

""This Earthling doesn't want to give the flower to us. What are we going to do?"

""Well this barbarian doesn't know about how to use it for bio-energy, and he doesn't even know its importance! Let's go: I will erase his memory of meeting you" said the youngest one who lifted his Asa Musa.

"Silem was against that, I appreciate. But I couldn't catch what he said."

"And what happened next?" asked my father anxiously. It was his first reaction for a good time – I thought he would have made known his views on this story a long time before this.

"Well, you remember, I was found sleeping near spring water later. Don't you" said Melis.

""I had always thought I had stepped onto something and fallen off. And last night in my dreams I finally saw how I landed near the spring water. The stranger took me there with his magic stick and left me. He said they would be back, and disappeared. I woke up and clearly heard a whisper: "We have arrived, come and see us … come… come…" That's why I take the sheep to Karala Aska while the "soul of the mountains" is growing."

"Oh my God!" -my father started praying and rocked back and forth, holding the collar of his shirt.

"My poor boy, you read too much. You have gone completely mad. Please do not tell me anymore. Drink some kymys. Always remember about God. Stop reading books. Come here: I will pray for you."

I was very angry even though I must have known how father would react. Like every Kyrgyz grown man I knew that elderly people should be respected and that parents are always right even when they don't believe you and cover you with manure. I calmed myself and with a quiet voice I told my father: "Steady father... I am going to the place where the "soul of the mountains" flourishes. Soon it will rain and then turn to snow and it is going to be stormy. Please speak kindly to your horse and go and round up the sheep. Then wait for me. If I haven't returned by this evening, then look for me at the spring!"

I got up and left. I put in my feet in the stirrups and started the climb to Karala Aska. As I looked back I saw my father was standing silent and motionless. As I started climbing I felt him staring at me. He obviously didn't understand my dream or my mission. Maybe he had other thoughts, but whatever was passing through his mind he didn't try to stop me.

It is difficult to describe how hard it is to climb to the place where "soul of the mountains" flourishes and grows. Maybe my body was well developed, as I have always been sporty and I grew accustomed to walking a lot while looking after sheep. Maybe it was my deep passion and strength of purpose that simply allowed me to reach the high mountains. As I climbed into the high mountains this time there was a strange absence of rain, wind, storm or snow, and I felt that instead of several gruelling hours in the saddle that we were on a casual stroll.

As I reached the place where I had fallen off last time I became aware that someone was sitting watching and waiting for me beside the big stone. I was a brave man and marched towards the person, but when I saw him my heart sank.

As I approached, the figure stood up, unrecognisable yet at the same time I still knew him. Though he looked different he had the same rubber soled footwear, but old and scuffed. He was wearing the old transparent raincoat and the same hat. His skin was as if stuck to his bones. His eyes were full of pulsing red veins: the eye white was almost gone. He had a dishevelled travel bag and his Asa Musa had turned to an ordinary dry old stick. Was it my stranger? I found myself doubting what I was seeing in front of me. It was very hard to believe it was the same stranger and I had to think hard to remember him. My subconscious appeared to have little doubt and I was amazed to hear myself enquiring "What happened   are you a beggar now?"

"Oh young man, do not be surprised.
You are in my destiny.
We met each other in very strange circumstances."

My beggar didn't even open his mouth but he was definitely singing a song to me, of that there was no doubt. The beggar continued singing as he had in my dreams last night, his mouth firmly closed as he sent me all this information telepathically (I was later to learn that this was a feat of mind control that allowed information to be transferred by bio-electrical power from brain impulses).

""Oh, Earth humanity!" my beggar said to me, continuing on his way."Last time we did wrong. We were punished when we returned to our planet. That flower lost its essential purpose: its primary quality has gone. The whole case was carefully researched by our galaxy's nineteen highest men at a meeting. They investigated the "soul of the mountains" down to the smallest molecule, and they discovered your genetic fingerprint on it, which characterises your whole body. This proved that the flower was stolen and revealed that the act of taking the flower was wrong. In our world, the philosophical and ethical law is the main and highest "morality" that we should obey. We submit and swear ourselves to this. As it is embedded in our beings, violating it means that any stolen objects lose their quality."

"As we grow up we simply know to obey this law. On our last visit we didn't even consider that our actions might have been unlawful, and so the big mistake occurred. I hadn't even thought about the details and principles of our ethical law before. Last time we were in a hurry and, of course, we overused our power, never thinking it could cause so much damage. We were wrong. Our ship's crew is no longer allowed to fly from the anti-world. Imagine: three thousand of our space agents now have to be retrained about our rights when we travel from our anti-world to the main space, as that number of agents should in every large space ship! When we reached the main world, the ship stayed in hyperspace inside orbit. From there landing ships, or flying saucers as you call them, fly to every star system. At the same time we have to stay out of hyperspace in orbits outside galactic orbits. The flying crew will be only three people in each flying saucer, and they will be expected to operate outside of galaxy orbits from hyperspace ships for an exact time only. Ships have to begin their flights to the main world exactly on time, and calculations should be correct to the millisecond, as space has its own stream, timetable and trajectory. If this were violated, the whole crew and the ship would not be able to reach their home. So that's why everything is different now. The main hyperspace ship wouldn't wait even milliseconds: any flying saucers which are late could get stuck, left in hyperspace outside orbit until next year. This means the crew would have to sleep in suspended animation for a whole year. Once they have been slept in suspended animation, they will be forbidden to fly to space forever.

"Last time we were in a hurry, because we were scared of what would happen. That's the reason. That's why the whole ship's crew who were supposed to fly to hyperspace was punished for making elementary mistakes. Now we no longer have the right to be spies. The mistakes we made are good example to the leaders of other, new expeditions, because we violated ethical law very clearly. The crew were punished harshly. The other two crew members – my friends – joined a new expedition which will research newborn stars, surrounded by dangerous radiation: they've been sent to one of the galaxy's nuclei."

"As for me, they sent me to ask or beg your forgiveness. That's why they sent me all by myself – to make sure you will really be happy. I have to be honest with you: if I'm unable to fulfil my orders I may stay on Earth forever. That's why I look like an Earth beggar. While we are bio-system-minded creatures, the main factor which alters our biology is our actions with respect to our ethical laws. As we carry out our tasks we change, based on whether we are doing right or not.

For example my clothing is not just that of an old beggar. This material is alive. This is given to us only once, when we are born. Thereafter it grows with us in a biological way. It reacts and changes to the environment and situation that we are in. If the weather is hot it gives us mildness, if it is cold it warms up. If there is no air it gives us oxygen. In short it is a skin spacesuit.

And it reflects everything we do, even if it is wrong. If we violate ethical law it gets old and the comfort starts to disappear. If you do good things it renews itself and looks always new and very comfortable. For example, if I violate ethical law my humanity diminishes and I reach the lowest level. I could even vanish - just vanish forever."

I felt sorry for the beggar. As I looked at him I ended up studying his stick. He noticed this, and continued singing his song into my head.

"And this is an Asa Musa- magic stick. We use them for movement like a main gravitation generator. Human have three times lower gravitation than us, my stick gives me equilibrium and stabilisation. We can also use them to reach our destinations in seconds through materialisation.

I was so tired and confused listening to all this from my beggar and I found it impossible to remember and understand everything. He noticed this and said "Did I not make myself and my punishment clear for you? Do I need to explain it all over again? "

The word punishment caught me by surprise, and I am sure I tilted my head in quizzical surprise as I asked "To make your punishment easier what should I do?"

"Forgive me!"

I was even more surprised! "How should I forgive you? For that flower, what is done is done. I have already forgotten that a long time ago." Poor beggar, I could easily say I forgave him if it was going to help him - it would cost me nothing to forgive him. Even people who make worse mistakes are forgiven! I thought for a moment then continued "If you are being honest and you really feel that you did wrong then I forgive you. My planet and I are not angry anymore," and I even smiled at my beggar.

At the moment that I told him this the beggar's old rubber boots immediately began to renew themselves, his old raincoat got bigger, but not totally new, his hat grew better and his old shoulder bag turned into a patchwork handmade bag. His Asa Musa turned into a better stick: not brilliant, but much better.

"You did forgive me but only for half of my mistake. For one of the other quarters, your father needs to thank me and forgive me: I need to meet him. And the last quarter is going to be hardest. To achieve that I need to do something really good for planet Earth."

Of course I was amazed. You should understand why. My father was never going to recognise that this beggar was from another world: a thirteen corner button imaginary galaxy! Put it the other way round: if he came from an anti-world how was he going to recognise this?

The really interesting part of his statement related to the fourth part of his redemption - something he should do for planet Earth – what could this be? When I asked he didn't even think a second and said "the Edelweiss! We are trying to earn the right to start to collect this flower all over again! I can teach you our ethical law!"

Was I really strong and brave enough to start arguing again with this beggar? What are they actually doing with that flower that is so bad? "I understand you perfectly" - said my beggar.

He had now turned into a better looking beggar!

"I will visit you tonight like a stranger. You are to act as if you do not recognise me. I have to meet your father and you and I will continue our conversation tomorrow at this place. You should go down now. Do not look so afraid, I will make a little snow and blow a little wind…

At that my beggar shook his Asa Musa up high and disappeared whilst I was mysteriously transported back.

My father and I let our sheep go and left them down the mountain at Tuura Bulak. It was already getting dark with the sky turning from light to dark blue as we got home. Near our house I saw a couple of horses tied up and I realised we had visitors.

As we entered our yurt there was the Farm Head Manager, along with the Farm Vet and the shepherds' postman sitting and drinking kymys. We greeted each other. After a few questions about how things were going the Farm Head stared at me and started.

"Melis, you are going to the city. They have started a new one-month course for master shepherds. I had hoped to send someone else but the shepherd I had in mind has given up life on the farm and has gone to the city to study at university or something" At that he turned and looked at my father with a big smile on his face. "For now old man you will be able to look after your sheep all by yourself." He carried on "Please go and take this course. You will be leaving tomorrow. There are seven or eight other young men also going from our Farm."

"I can't go!" I said with passion. I had never liked how this Farm chief dealt with people. He always talked with smiles but had something else in mind. Every second word was not true. He never kept his word. Last winter he promised to bring our wintering pasture extra hay and food but nothing ever arrived. Our sheep were so thin that I had to ask the village head for extra help. Later, in an open Communist party meeting I was very critical of him and that's why he is always against me. I always feel he is looking for my weakness but I have always made sure he couldn't find any mistakes in my work. Looking at him now, he had come at the wrong time. He was smiling with his white teeth but I knew inside his mind would be working against me.

"In spring time that you gave us that lazy assistant to us to help when we had to do the lambing. After you gave us school kids – they weren't any help. And my father was too busy to take care of all this as well. Now, if I go to shepherd school the government sheep left for my father to look after will be too much for him. Go and find another foolish person to send. It would be better say that we should leave all these sheep under open sky…"

"Whoa, whoa, young man... Easy... easy. Why you are being so noisy? I am trying to do you a favour, and you don't like it? You will go to the city, enjoy it and learn a lot about how to look after our sheep. The lambs could be managed just as well without you! Your parents will be the main managers after the new main shepherd leaves. He has been sent by the special commission, he'll separate the new lambs and go."

"Oh shut up, don't act that you came from the sky" I was not very patient, and he was annoying me.

"When lambs are born, you will just count the dead or ill ones while I am not here. You will make up stories so that you could take away the nice, living ones for yourself, and make me responsible for all the losses.

Tell me that you came to stop me being the head shepherd – do not twist the facts!"

"If you do not want to be head shepherd, then fine. It is up to you" said the farm chief directly, smiling but not with his eyes but with poison on his face. We will continue this conversation later. He start laying into me that everyone had a hundred and seventy lambs. "You never had more than a hundred and forty. Where are the other lambs? Are you hiding them? Are you stealing them? Don't be foolish. We will be hearing your case soon young man"

"If you think you're a God holding the sky you may drop it on me!" I stood up "Who has a hundred and seventy lambs? Kurmash and Chykmash? They're your brothers you're talking about."

He had me riled and I couldn't help but continue "Who is giving them the best summer places and the warm winter places? Who is giving them both extra hay and food in winter? Who is adding extra private lambs to deceive you and receive accolades? We have eyes and saw everything, we have ears and heard everything; we have brains to work it out. I will reveal your true face hiding from honesty, and soon it will be over.

46

"Your words speak for themselves!" he stood up to stare at me with his kamchy[9] in his hand "If you don't have proof I will sue you – you should know that!"

"Stop! You are like little children, stop it now!" my father said. The postman, an older man, nodded in agreement. The vet was very quiet and went out from the yurt with a sarcastic smile. We all followed him out. I started walking away to go and look after our sheep.

"Hey, help them get onto their horses!" said my father.

"Just leave them, they have legs and arms and they can help themselves. We didn't invite them…"

I was a bit sorry, remembering the saying "don't burn your cloth just because you have a little louse". I'd forgotten my fight was just with the farm head, and I had accused everyone. At least I should help the old postman. But what is done is done – they had left…

My father stared into my eyes. He walked quickly, untied the postman's horse and pulled the horse away to help old post man got in his horse. When the others got on their horses and rode away to the other village, our dog Koorochy chased them for miles, barking loudly.

I stood up and, lost in thought, did not notice my father approaching me his moustache and beard twitching. He was so angry he whipped me with his kamchy. I wasn't expecting this

"You are a son of a bitch. You've never been well behaved. . When have you see any other Kyrgyz fighting with guests and showing them the door? You know that even if a black snake comes to your house you should spray it white to encourage it to go away peacefully. You never respect your ancestors' traditions, you bastard. If it ever happens again I will kill you myself.

He didn't look at me at all. Damn: my father didn't understand that this was the only way to talk with the farm head.

I don't even know why I cried: because he was on the boss's side or because he had whipped me. I turned my back to him as I realised my tears were flowing. It was only the third time in my life my father had been so angry that he had whipped me.

---

[9] Horse whip

The first time he had threatened to kill me. When I was nine I stole my classmate's football. He found out and he said if I ever stole anything in my life or told lies he would chop my arms and tongue off. He whipped me but I didn't cry.

When I graduated from school we had argued about religion. He whipped me again and threw me out of the house, but I didn't cry.

Did I cry now because my father had whipped me or because the farm head had been cruel to me as usual? There had been much tougher and bigger disappointments in my life when I hadn't cried at all. When I fell off my horse my arms had been injured badly and broken my leg, and I had lain in an empty field for two days before I was found. Even then I did not cry. I was only six years old at the time. I could not move my arms to chase flies away from my eyes. Oh, I had been very angry? Even when I won a local competition and then took part in the whole State competition, but only came in a mid-ranking position, that hadn't been enough to make me cry. I'll never forget how disappointed I was in myself, I'll never ever forget it, but even then there had been no tears. So why now? Maybe I was crying because I was afraid of the farm head who was threatening me? No, of course, not!

Maybe I was crying because there were so many stupid, selfish and very slow people in life who really disappointed me but seemed to get into positions of power.

I pulled myself together, washed my face in crystal clear spring water, and went out after the sheep which had now strayed far from our house. The sun was already down, and I still had to guide the sheep back home.

When I reached my sheep they were far away in Besh Moinok village. Besh Moinok village was very strange in itself. From outside it looks like the palm of my hand with five hills. If you accidently go to one of the corners, it is hard to find the other end. You will wander like a partridge and will take a whole day to find your way out.

This place is good for shepherding on rainy days. The wind and rain is tempered by the five hills, and it has been very warm and quiet there for so many years.

I rounded up all the sheep from a hard-to-access corner before I turned back. The sun was already setting behind the Karala Aska and as I reached home it was getting very dark.

My father met me, and seems he was very worried, after asking me, why I was late, he start talking to me with calm voice. He jumped off from his horse and helped me to herd the sheep ready for the night.

As I approached our Yurt my father was still talking "...I should have helped him earlier." He then addressed me "Look now, we have a very respectable guest in our house, and all you can do is to herd the sheep. You used to get crazy when you saw very religious people: you used to have an itchy tongue. Please be normal and polite, do not behave badly and show him respect. We have a God loving creature in our house. A beggar!"

"What?"

"Oh, what is wrong with you, you silly boy…"

"No, nothing…" I had totally forgotten about Silem. "It has been a long time since we last saw a beggar in this region. He must be lost, poor thing?" I said.

"He is not an ordinary beggar" said my father in something close to a whisper. "He is a saintly one. Maybe he is Saint Aleikumsalam himself! Long, long ago I used to dream of him, he used to advise me. Now he is in our house. He wouldn't come to just any house: only honest believers and those who will accept him with all their hearts can receive him as a guest. Just when I thought you were ill or upset, the holy Lord blessed you himself. I wasn't paying attention when you were mumbling about your dream about a beggar. God will forgive me even if I whipped you: it was that head of the farmer's fault."

My father was trying to make jokes to cheer me up and he was being rather funny. I wanted to laugh.

I imagined that Silem was worried about if my father would recognise that I already knew him and was the alien from my story. If my father recognised that it was him, would he realise that he had to thank him and forgive him so that his guilt would be three quarters forgiven. Would he then address the fourth part of his guilt? It is very strange that they even have their ethical laws as well. It had started me thinking.

Do I have to give them permission to take our Soul of the Mountain? How? I can't myself be responsible for the whole planet? That poor thing, he told me on behalf of his whole planet for the planet's boys and girls to make it worthwhile, what the essence of the flower was. We never dreamed that the poor thing would fly such a long way just to steal our flowers? It is very strange that they even have ethical laws. What if I start using their ethical laws and keep Silem on Earth forever? Maybe in the end he will work for me as a shepherd! He has a human-like nature as well! When will we stop just thinking about ourselves? Of course, there are so many herbs and flowers on our mountains and it wouldn't be wrong to stop a human being flying back to his homeland just because he pulled out one flower? Would it?

To use this circumstance and curtail someone else's freedom is total nastiness! No, we are humanity on Earth, and to behave like that just does not suit us. Of course, it doesn't!

After we settled our sheep in the shed my father caught one of the spring lambs that belonged privately to our family, and passed it to me.

"The fruit of real honest hard work – we should slaughter it for our most respected visitor," my father started to pray in a whisper and it looked like he was praying for our beggar. I smiled inside and nearly told him: "Father, it is the other way around, he is supposed to ask forgiveness from you!" but I didn't say anything.

I didn't want to disappoint my father so I opened the yurt door and let him go in first. I followed him with the lamb. I saw Silem, who was now sitting in the place reserved for important visitors, He looked much better than he had done: his face and cheeks were pinker and his coat looked almost new again. Being received into my fathers' household had given him the redemption he sought and his whole physical being was now almost back to its original self.

"Asalaam Alaykum!, warm greetings" I said, and winked at Silem. He winked back at me.

"Valeykuum Asalaam! Warm greetings too" he said and took the lamb from me. "Gods little creature, be blessed: the good Lord will help him be happier!" He stood up to whisper something, rolled his eyes, started praying and said "Amen" and then passed the blessed lamb back to me.

Father was on his knees and mother said "Amen" in support.

I was so amazed and was wondering "Is he the same Silem who flew here from another planet, or is he a real beggar, who got lost in these mountains?"

Silem sent me telepathic messages, because he saw how lost I looked. "I will explain everything to you tomorrow, but for now, you should do everything that your father tells you."

It was becoming too much for me, and I knew I wanted to be alone to think things through and get some fresh air. I blurted out, "Father, I forgot my binoculars near the spring. I should go and fetch them, please slaughter the lamb yourself." I was about to continue with "Father pray first and then I'll go" but when he saw my eyes were bright and shiny he kept his silence and nodded his head to give his permission for me to go out. He took the lamb from me.

When I got back home, there was a three legged iron stand on the fire and our big kazan on top. It was about three quarters full of boiling water and the fresh lamb meat. My mother was sitting patiently beside the kazan, skimming the excess fat off the boiling water with a sieve. This way of cooking is employed thousands of times a day throughout Central Asia.

Father and the beggar were finished their tea and they had just started telling long, long stories. It looked like the conversation was just beginning, as my father had just started his life story.

"... then after I retired, we came over here to spend the rest of our lives. For the first two or three years we were building a house. It was impeccable when we finished. Our move to the mountains blessed us with lovely isolation, and my wife and I used to sit watching the sun set every day, and then we had little else to do but wait until it rose again the next morning. We got so bored. I eventually went to the collective farm head to ask for some sheep to look after..."

"Old man, aren't you tired of sheep? You are now over sixty! Now is the time for young people, you would be better as a watchman," they said when I first asked. I had looked after horses all my life; I didn't do any other job in my life. I cannot stare at the walls like an old dog. "If you want me to do something – give me some animals to look after. If you want to help me, help me then! Otherwise, I will go somewhere else where they will help me," I told them stubbornly.

"They got tired of me and told me "Don't even dream of looking after horses. If you can find a young shepherd who can start in the autumn to help you, we will give you a whole group of lambs from our collective farm."

"Deal!" I said. I had a nephew that could drive tractors, but not as well as he should, I had to agree to him being the main shepherd and me being his assistant. When he gave up his tractor, he was so skinny he nearly dropped dead. But it is in our Kyrgyz nature… after three or four years, he had learned everything – he was a great shepherd, and looked after the sheep so well. He then got married and fathered three sons. Now he is the head shepherd and his sons are among the best shepherds. They haven't been losing any lambs; they look after them so well in their two pastures. Now he doesn't even have any space left in his chest, because of his gold 'Best Shepherd' medals!

"I was stubborn as well, and looked after sheep myself. During the hardship of winter and early spring, my nephew always helped me. Every summer we used to go to Song Kul - the high mountain spring water lake. I enjoyed looking after horses there very much. My wife and I cannot live without drinking kymys. Now we have my nephew's mare, for milking and making our own kymys to drink. My nephew prefers buttered whey for his kymys, so we give him our cow for milking."

My father then looked over at me, busy stoking the fire with dried cow pats, He pointed at me with his chin and continued "We were so busy moving around and working hard with the animals in the mountains that he went to boarding school. That was just as well, as he is so stubborn, never listening to anyone's opinion. Damn boy.

He reads books all the time, that's all he's good for. When he finished school, we asked him to help us but he just wanted to continue studying. His mother took his side and both were very argumentative about it so I left them to decide. He went to the city and failed Medical Institute exams, but instead he went to the Sports Institute to be a "Wrestler"… Oh, God bless them, this Government: they are so strange, aren't they? Teaching students how to fight, and actually giving them financial support, what a carry on! It would be better to teach them how to look after sheep. Yes, after five years of study all they know is how to put gel in their hair and hold a folder that says: A male sheep is a ram, sheep can breed and they produce mutton. That's all they know. That vet used to say the same, but now he thinks that he is cleverer than all of us." My father was laughing sweetly.

"Not long ago I was gathering in my sheep in the spring when I got caught in an avalanche. I was on my horse, just below the peak of the mountain and was just beginning to collect my sheep when five or six mountain goats appeared from nowhere, springing through the snow. At the same time I saw two or three dogs, and three men on horseback. One of them jumped off his horse and shot the goats. The loud "boom" echoed all around. After what seemed like an eternity the high mountainside where the goats were started moving all of a sudden. I knew I was watching an avalanche. Either the loud noise of the gun or the goats' feet had set off the snow. I quickly shooed off my flock of sheep before I heard the snow bearing down on me. The avalanche hit my horse and we were moving backwards. My poor animal started screaming. I remember how I then flew away from the horse like a hat flies off your head in the wind."

My mother was wiping her tears away as she sat quietly listening to the story again. She then picked up where my father had stopped "At that time the bastard (my mother started calling the Farm head that after that day) came to tell me that my husband had been hit by an avalanche. I was in shock: I didn't really know what to do so I grabbed a shovel and ran like crazy to search the field. What a stupid idea, where was I and where was the field?" said my mother who had started smiling

"Yes, what a bastard" I said. No-one flinched as I castigated the farm head. It seemed that before I came home, my parents had told the beggar about my fight with the farm head and my antipathy towards him.

My father intervened. "Why was he there? It seems he was returning after checking up on three winter fields, when he accidentally saw those goats."

I said, still holding my head down and staring at the fire, I said "Any good man knows that they should not hunt and shoot in the mountains when the snow is prone for avalanche. Yet he was carrying a gun! He had obviously been hunting."

"No-one knows that," my father looked at me with his calm eyes.

As if to draw a line under the story and the bad feelings it evoked, he turned to the beggar. "Holy man, please, would you care for another cup of tea?"

"Bless you! I have had enough. We should say Amen", said my father's holy man.

My father said "Amen" and my beggar said a very long prayer after which my mother started cleaning the table and the tablecloth.

I noticed again that the beggar was touching his big finger on his right or left hands when he was holding his stick. The index finger looked boneless, smooth with just flesh, but somehow stuck to his stick.

But when he was praying with his fingers spread wide, he moved his stick away; I didn't see how he managed to hold it with his knees.

"Holy man, please make yourself comfortable. You can stretch your legs if you wish. Would you like a pillow rest for your arm and elbow?" my mother said as she walked towards the pile of blankets.

"Ah, yes, yes please." said the beggar and he nodded his head.

I was watching this whole animation theatre and laughed accidently. I looked towards my father:

"May I go out and looked after our sheep?" I said, going outside. I felt so strange. In this area there is no one who is educated and smart. When I am surrounded by country people, I get really annoyed. When I am surrounded by old people I feel just like a child. Even if I knew everything I could never control myself.

There were so many stars out in the sky and the moon was only just visible, though it was shining brightly as well. On the other side there is the village of horses. I could even hear young boys and girls playing Ak cholmok, searching for a hidden piece of bone. Far away I could hear someone singing a song of snores. On another side a jealous stallion's snoring was clearly audible. Our sheep were lying comfortably, some still chewing grass, some searching anxiously for their lambs.

A group of young lambs were running around in the place where I used to relax. There were a few small waves on Lake Song Kol but otherwise it was calm. It was a sweet night on the jailoo, and Mother Nature was throwing happiness and kindness all around, and life was accepting it and carrying it well and proud.

Our yurt was pitched in the midst of the mountains, and a little light came under the bottom. As the soft wind blew, it clearly carried the sounds of people talking within and then, as it ebbed, the sounds would drift off to nothing. It sounded like father was telling his story about how he survived the avalanche.

He had been moving with the power of the avalanche down the mountainside when all of a sudden father dropped into a crevasse. The snow kept moving down the mountain for many more miles while my father ended up sitting in the bottom of the crevasse, amazed he was alive. As he looked up he realised that the sides were too smooth to climb out down the crevasse all he could see was melt water that was so dark and cold that he dared not move. Luckily there was a dry cave under one side of the crevasse which provided a refuge of sorts for him as he found himself cut off from the mountainside above.

The search for my father went on for almost two days but he could not be found. The exhausted teams even asked a specialist to come and help with his radar, yet still they could not find him.

While near the crevasse a couple of kids, who were tagging along with their fathers in the search party, crawled up to the edge of the crevasse. Needless to say, their fathers' express instructions that it was dangerous and that they shouldn't go near the crevasse had only spurred them on to see what mysteries it held. Whilst they were looking down from the top of the crevasse they were amazed to see my father wandering about at the bottom like a little ant. The kids quickly got help and a couple of young athletic men soon got a strong rope in place and hauled my injured father back onto the mountain.

We had all been sitting praying to God. When I heard the news I was beside myself with relief and, as the team brought my father back to the village my first words to him were to tell him: "That's enough, now I will be the head shepherd!"

As I came back into the yurt my father continued the story "Well, he gave up his Institute of Sport and became a shepherd. After that he went to do his military service. I thought that afterwards he would start studying, not look after sheep. But in the last two or three years, he's been away once in the winter and once in the summer to take exams. He studied externally from home to become a poet. The only thing that's wrong is that he is not married yet. While I am still alive, I would really like to see him married, and before I pass away I would like to kiss my grandchildren." My father wiped away his tears.

"Inshallah," said the beggar, praying at the same time "may your son's way be open and may God help him to be a happy man."

Father and mother said "Amen" together as mother arranged her headscarf correctly.

My mother wasn't one to be shy, and she stared at the beggar as she often looks at me when it seems like she is talking to herself. Quietly she started talking "Oh, a long time ago, before last year, there was such a beautiful girl, she visited us once. She was with Melis's other friends. Then my dear boy told me that this was my future daughter-in-law, and that she wanted to meet me personally. That was the happiest moment in my life. Poor me, it was so unexpected that I could not think what to cook for them. She had nice long hair and seemed very intelligent. Things got spoilt however, as she was upset because of some little plant. Poor girl, she was crying her eyes out, cuddling me and wanting to tell me something, but she couldn't. I guess I simply cannot understand the younger generation these days."

The beggar and I were staring at each other. He was so uncomfortable that he put his head down. Nobody noticed that we secretly knew each other's thoughts.

Father was staring at the fire. Strangely, mother was making a noise with the coins of her hair ornament and she went to the kitchen area of the yurt to start making noodles. Mother was almost twenty years younger than father, and she always looked very young to me. Now I watched her trying to make noodles, her old fingers slowly daubing the flour with splashes of salted water. The whole picture made me cry.

I should get married. I should make my mother's life easier, and bring a wife who will help her with all her domestic chores. First I had to think of her. Secondly - who should I think of as my wife? Of course, Rena! What was my maxim, whom had I always thought that I would present the "Soul of the Mountain" to – I could still do it – or was I too late? I had always thought of bringing the flower to my true love as she slept near spring water and that as she awoke she would be overjoyed and proud to see me acting like a real man. If I didn't do it in a manly fashion, she would never marry me. I would have to be pure in my intentions. Now of course I cannot give the flower to Rena, as I had promised myself I would.

I turned my face to the beggar. He was staring at me; I noticed his jaw drop a little, as if he had understood all my inner thoughts! Then it dawned on me, he was reading my entire impulsive mind.

After eating our dinner of the fresh cooked lamb, we started preparing to sleep. "I would like to sleep outside, beside Melis. Please make two separate sleeping places for us," requested the beggar "I am used to sleeping in the open in the wild forest and fields, if I can't see the stars I cannot sleep at all!"

I understood that Silem was trying to get a chance to talk to me.

"No problem holy man," said my father as he turned to my mother. "Please prepare soft and warm blankets for the holy man, wife.... There are plenty of mattresses." Then, after a moment's silence he added, "Please, may I join our holy man, put something there for me too. I think I would like to talk all night, if you don't mind."

I understood my father too. He was wondering. "Was this beggar sent by God, will I ever see him again?" He was trying so hard to be hospitable, to show him the deepest of respect. Maybe he wasn't meant to share his entire life story from beginning to end, but he wanted to share it and share it honestly with this man who had come along, particularly if he really was a holy man.

I was helping to prepare our sleeping place, and brought two piles of blankets from the yurt to the top of the pasture. It was a spot I had relaxed and slept in many times. Father was watching how it was done for the holy man, making sure his sleeping place was good. After we finished making a place to sleep for ourselves, my mother went back to our yurt, firstly covering its crown, before disappearing inside and extinguishing the lamp.

It was a near-full moon that shone smoothly in the dark sky. In the moonlight Lake Song Kol looked so magnificent, with small waves shining through the dark like sparks. Nature with all its holiness, the grandeur of it all ran through my body like electricity and my heart was beating in my chest, pumping blood through my body. The feelings and the image of Song Kol were so strong that a song started to explode from within me. I don't remember when I wrote this song: it was a long time ago, when my world was a wild one.

Wind is blowing smoothly onto my face...
Bright summer night at Song Kol.
Stars are playing, chasing each other
They fall down from space, to Lake Song Kol

Young stallion calling in the field,
Turning the other horses back home.
One stallion from the herd is screaming with victory:
"Don't come along to the green field ..."

The crested owl screams,
Looking for food and hooting.
The moon is beautiful and smiling in the sky

The gorge is dressed in white 'Elechek'.
In the green field the cows still graze,
After stuffing themselves all day with lush green grass
The dog starts, wakes and barks loudly
Disturbing the slumbering pasture…

Sheep are drowsy in the barn…
The lonely song of the bird
Echoes again and again

Fairytale summer night at Song Kol
Fresh wind blowing from the shore
Stars are falling down to Song Kol;
Splashing the water and playing happily…

Far, far away you can hear the lilting voice of a bird, from time to time singing loud in the field, but then fading into silence.

The sheep were drowsy and were settling down for the night. Around me I was surrounded by the nature of the Ala Too Mountains. Beside me two star ambassadors representing two entirely different worlds, two quite opposite parallels of each other, were sweetly talking. They are holy to each other. The only person who knows the truth is me and I am keeping the secret. As I am the only person who knows it, I may even have the right to judge them both.

One of them is crystal clear like an innocent child; like the clear night of the Tian-Shan Mountains. His conviction is like an honest open field! The other is messing with the minds of people. He has secrets. He can't make a decision on the ethical law, poor miserable chap. One of them talks whilst the other one listens. How did this connection start?

Lying on my back, staring at the moon I listened: what are they talking about? The ambassadors of two worlds, instead of sweetly sleeping in nice, clean white sheets were lying on their duvets with their clothes on. They were using their arms as pillows now and were talking deeply, far away in their memories.

Their stories played out in front of my eyes like a colourful film in the air. Some of the pictures were very familiar to me.

CHAPTER 3
STORY OF MY FATHER

Who is this?!
A ripe red apple
With all his heart,
Supporting you and me,
Standing as an open flame,
Wishing you the highest achievements in life...

My father was a good storyteller and I listened intently as the three of us lay on our blankets. He started by setting the scene of his early working life.

"In the early fifties the Suusamyr area was separated off from Jumgal district, and became part of Chuy Province. It was a busy time for Kyrgyzstan and its agricultural areas, which were constantly being re-organised into large collective farms to be run by the Soviet Government.

After Suusamyr became part of Chuy Province, all its small villages and mountain farms were united with the large collective farms of the wide and fertile Chuy Valley, providing them with high summer pastures for their sheep, cows and horses.

Suusamyr was very wild with open fields; a cold wind blew from Kapchygai in the south and when it died it was replaced with a strong but milder wind from the Koko Meren River to the northwest. The cold, still, all-permeating fogs of the Chuy Valley with its Koko Meren River never rose to Suusamyr. Even the south side of the highest mountains in Suusamyr never experienced the biting cold weather found on the main collective farm in the valley.

It was, though, a notoriously difficult area to access. Nevertheless, the Government invested in the area. That spring, transporter vehicles carrying new hay cutting machines were already crossing the new bridge over the Koko

Meren River: it had previously been such a dangerous crossing and had been swept away many times by the spring flood, so that only a mountain goat could reach the places where the grass had been cut. Now the transporters could reach the hay, which had been piled up by combine harvesters beside the streams.

At the Ak Kurchoo collective farm on one of the highest pastures there wasn't enough space in the main building for us all to stay in winter. However, it was so cold that it was not practical to stay in yurts. Half of us were sent to lodge at a place which they called Aidarkan's Winter Palace. The antiquarian winter animal sheds were rebuilt, and we installed fireplaces in the old buildings.

Initially it was only locals who stayed in the Suusamyr area over the winter. Everyone else went away, as the winter was very harsh. As the years progressed and the buildings were steadily improved however, the area gradually became more pleasant to live in.

I knew this place so well and I had a really good rapport with Danilchenko, the boss. With his encouragement, and also aware that the Government was making inspections, I decided to take my own exams as well. I was soon asked to move to the mountain pasture at Suusamyr myself, and they gave me three more men to help me out. I chose them myself; they were young and tough and had the enthusiasm of youth.

For the first month, my three young helpers were scared. Every day I took one of them to train and to show how to look after the horses at night. Once they had learned everything, they liked looking after the animals by themselves and became very confident young men. We decided to take turns looking after the animals for a week at a time.

And so when autumn arrived that year, we were among those planning to stay in Suusamyr for the winter, after all the others had gone with their animals to the Chuy Valley.

The only ones left in the central building were the people, and animals which would be fed only by hay – herds of horses, of cows and a flock of five hundred sheep. We were due to spend the winter with our first horse herd.

The Government had ruled that we were supposed to let the horse herd go to the snowy fields during the day, and feed them with hay in the evenings. To look after them this way was madness, as the constant change from inside to outside would make the animals hungry; spend more energy, lose confidence and weight, meaning they could easily not survive until spring.

For me and the others who used to spending winter here, this was already clear. That's why even when there were forecasts of minus 45 degrees or more for Suusamyr the horses were left in the open field. Both during the day and during the night when they were left outside, beside the house or the mountains, however they did need continual checking.

When the other young men came over from head office – because it was winter and they were supposed to give my young boys some time off every other month – the training and courage of my young men shone through. When we let them try to look after the herds we soon discovered how naïve and soft they were: giving only water to the horses at night and letting them walk aimlessly around the fields wasting valuable energy against the cold with only cold water in their bellies then letting them come into the buildings to sleep in the warmth."

Having set the scene I knew my father's mind well, and knew he would recount the story of Seyit.

One of these young men from the head office was called Seyit, and he used to help watch the horses at night. He was returning from Sasyk Bulak by fording Koko Meren River: easy, given the low water level. It seems he had private business in that area. He was only twenty three, still young and full of fire and bravado. He used to ride very fast and had a beautiful horse!

I was already fast asleep after drinking Bozo[10]. A ghostly figure arrived with a magic stick and was yelling at me: "Hey, damn you, you've gone and fallen asleep. Wake up! Seyit was trying to cross Koko Meren River and fell off his horse. He is now lying in an open field and really needs your help. Go, Go!" and then the ghost disappeared.

When I woke up fully, I thought it was a dream. I wasn't sure – maybe it was, maybe not: maybe my dream was true. Just in case I decided to ride my horse and pushed on through the snow towards Sasyk Bulak. As I approached the river crossing just before the village I found Seyit. He was lying in shallow water with his horse walking around him because the bridle was in Seyit's hands. He had tried to make the horse pull him out of the water but it couldn't and instead kept coming back to him.

---

[10] A traditional alcoholic drink made from boiled, fermented millet

It seemed he had crossed the Koko Meren River after leaving Sasyk Bulak. The river never froze, but the banks on both sides were always covered in ice. Apparently, in trying to ford, his horse had slipped, and as it slipped it crushed one of his legs. It looked like the leg was broken, and he was struggling to stand on the other one. I helped Seyit up and got him into the open field where I wrapped up his foot in a feed bag and hauled him back onto his horse. Together we crossed the Koko Meren, and I led him up the road to the village.

As we finally reached the village I told him "The third last house in the village is Turusbek's. You should get to know him: he is an herbalist. Last year he celebrated his grandson's birthday and we played a game of Ulak Tartysh[11]. He has a very white beard and is truly an Aksakal[12] of the highest order. He should be able to help you. Can you ride?"

Seyit was a young man with spirit. "Sure, old man! Of course I can ride myself; please go back to look after the animals. If my leg is broken I will get him to tie it up correctly: if I have just pulled it out of joint then I will get him to make sure he pulls it back. If any bones are broken then I will ask him to apply shak-shak[13]. I will be back before bed time!" After this, he whipped his horse into a gallop.

What a young man!

He had gone to find Turusbek, only to discover that he wasn't there but had gone to Jumgal to visit his friend. Seyit then rode straight to the Central Office building for our area, not even getting off his horse once. It was a long ride.

In those days there were fewer doctors and they lacked experience. The duty doctor could not help him, so contacted Frunze[14] by radio to ask for help. This arrived in the form of a helicopter, which took Sevit to a hospital in the city. I heard later that it didn't work out: his leg went bad with gangrene and had to be amputated just below the hip.

My father paused in deep thought and Silem and I both stared at him, wondering whether to speak. Then, after a deep sigh, he continued:

"After Seyit fell off his horse and went to Frunze to be treated I had to look after the whole herd by myself. As the herd went to the fresh field I decided to have a nap: it was still dark in the early morning, with only the moon and stars lighting up the field. I tied two bridles together and then bundled the ropes under myself:

---

[11] A traditional game played on horseback where two teams on horseback have to get a dead goat carcass to a target
[12] Wise man. Those who carry a white beard do so as a symbol of old age and wisdom that is given great respect in Kyrgyz society. In Kyrgyz Ak is white and Sakal is beard
[13] A herb often applied to bone injuries
[14] Now Bishkek - the capital of Kyrgyzstan

this gave my horse a chance to wander around a little and forage for fresh green grass or lichen in the snow. For a man alone in the open field, having a nap is very dangerous. Suddenly, just as I was drifting off to sleep, I was woken by a loud commotion and shrieking from all the horses.

My own horse was upset and was digging into the earth with its front hooves. The other horses had all formed a big circle.

That year the snow had been really deep, winter had been harsh and the wolves were wild and hungry. From time to time, we heard how in other villages wolves had taken a horse or a sheep. Our village had somehow survived the winter without any such losses. People used to tell stories about how I kept fires going all night long and never slept. But in reality, I just used to keep quiet and pray to the Almighty.

I never thought our horses were special. The main stallion, Kambar Ata[15], was a very light blue colour. Such a beautiful and fine animal!

One day in late autumn it had been raining, and we'd been so busy running around trying to round up the horses we didn't realise they were tired, wet and exhausted. It got to the point that they began to refuse to walk and go where we wanted. We all dismounted and walked ourselves, utterly miserable in the wet and not at all sure what to do. Suddenly all the horses stopped and we heard the voice of a stallion, and through the rain we saw him walking towards us. We all stood in the rain waiting. In that wild and windy weather the horse that approached us was strong and walked easily against the driving rain: his hair was long and beautiful and shone an almost blue white. He came to us all alone. I was so happy - even happier than when my son was born. I took the saddle off my own horse and he let me rig it on his back and immediately let me mount and ride him. And this blue white stallion ran like the light from a shining star, and behind him the other horses followed: their tiredness forgotten all the way to Kapchygai.

On arrival I had to work hard to stop the other exhausted horses and to calm them I had to keep calling "shush-shush". Before we even started the run to Kapchygai, black night arrived - we were blinded and couldn't see a thing. And that's when I saw for the first time how my blue-white stallion's ears shone like two candle flames. This was a big help for the other horses and allowed me to herd at night in the big and open fields.

The other horse men wanted to make him run in competitions or even ride him in

---

[15] A typical name for a pedigree horse

games of Ulak Tartysh, but I forbade them from riding him or even coming close to this special horse. I made it known that if I ever saw anyone riding this stallion I would kill them and push their body into the Koko Meren River. Although I often had to repeat my threat, it seemed to have the desired effect. This aristocratic animal, Kambar Ata of the horses, how could anyone ride a Lord for a game?

When I woke to that horrific noise, I immediately jumped onto my horse and rode over to where the whole herd was now standing in a circle. I forced my way to the centre where I found a mare lying covered in blood. As I dismounted and placed my hand on her neck I discovered she was struggling to breathe. As I looked up I saw a large grey wolf lying motionless nearby and realised it too was dead. Through a gap between the horses' legs I noticed something lurking in the deep dark night. As I got back on my horse I saw that it was running away and rode straight after it. As I peered into the night I thought the creature was probably a lone wolf, but it was casting a strong shadow. Then when it reached a patch of white snow and with the stars shining brightly in the clear night sky, I realised there were three wolves. I then remembered that I had a hunting gun on my shoulder, and I brought it round and shot into the air a couple of times. By now most of the herd had moved away from the dying mare and were still agitated. Then a horse, with its two ears lit up like candles, went into the herd and they steadied and calmed.

I rode back over to the poor dying mare and knelt with her until she drew her last breath. Then I walked over to the dead wolf and lit a match. The creature's head was smashed to pieces and horse hoof marks could easily be seen on the crushed bone and fur.

I rode my horse back to the herd. I could sense that the animals were scared, but they had gathered round the horse with lit-up ears. At first I thought it was my blue-white stallion, but it wasn't him. As I stared and my eyes got used to both the night and the markings and styles of the herd, I realised it was a skinny mare I had always thought of as peripheral to the herd. Yet here she was, with the same ears as my blue-white stallion, bringing calmness and courage to the herd. That was her! Oh, God! And I started praying. I thought about this poor skinny mare, how I had always wanted to leave her in the barn rather than bring her to graze on the lush green grass. But she was special as well! As I searched the area I couldn't find my blue-white stallion. It was only later that I heard his loud neighing and saw him. He was coming down through the Kyrchyndy Badal from far Ych- Kyngoi, and his two ears were still shining like candles. As the blue-white stallion approached and then entered the herd, the skinny mare's ears dimmed and then their light was gone.

Later that night, the herd had reunited but spread out over an area to graze. The mare started kicking snow and, even though her ears were no longer lit up, she was trying to control the herd. The blue-white stallion was grazing well away from the herd and raised his head when the horses all started neighing. The herd only calmed down after the blue-white stallion arrived back. Then they started searching for more grass...

After this, I always looked after the herd myself and I always paid special attention to the blue-white stallion, and the little mare.

At dusk, the blue-white stallion leaves the herd, and his ears light up. When the sky is full of stars the little mare goes to the other side of the herd and her ears also light up. Then the stallion returns to the herd and starts grazing. I gradually understood that we weren't attacked by wolves because of these lights. I also understood the rumours that I used lighting all night long to look after my herd.

My ancestors knew of this and this was why they always looked after these fine animals and why I had heard many stories about Kambar Ata, a horse who brings only good luck to his owner. I had lived half a century and had never come across such an animal until then.

When I remember my blue-white stallion, I cry. If I had done something else with my life other than working with horses maybe I would have better stories to tell."

Father was nervous and he wiped tears from his eyes: poor old man. He was silent for a time.

"Melis!" he shouted my name. "Are you asleep? If not, listen to my story. I am telling it so you can hear as well."

I turned onto my stomach, lit a cigarette and stared straight at him so that he could see I was listening to everything he was telling me.

"After spring has passed and summer begins, when the grass turns lush green, there is a plant which appears that we call 'dancing grass'[16] if an animal eats it, it falls ill for some reason. What is 'dancing grass'? What is it for? I really don't know what use this grass is when it turns green. It's a strange plant – it can rustle even when there is no wind, looking like it is dancing. Only local

---

[16] Author's note: In my opinion 'dancing grass' is a special drug that causes drowsiness. It only affects some parts of an animal's brain. We know that meat from animals (especially horses) that have been driven insane by 'dancing grass' is still edible and does not affect humans in any way.

herbalists understood what it was. They hated 'dancing grass', it made them very angry and they used to pull it out. It usually grew in wild fields, but only seemed to grow sometimes. Usually wild white mice eat it. If these mice are eaten by foxes, wolves, or badgers they go mad.

If a foal tastes this grass it runs like crazy for two or three days. If someone notices the foal and takes it, exhausted, to a waterfall and ties it up, the fat covering its eyes will go away and its craziness will pass.

I never heard what happens if a cow eats this 'dancing grass', if it goes crazy or not, and I have never seen either. If a lamb eats it, it will bounce around like a ball and eventually die. One old man told me that if a horse eats 'dancing grass' it will always be slow and so miserable that it will keep searching for something it never finds and will be left behind by the main herd. The best thing to do with it is to have it slaughtered, as it would still be edible.

It was late afternoon, the sun was shining bright, but there were no flies around. I was trying to help a new young foal to suckle and my wife was milking some mares. She had just finished with one and was moving to another when we suddenly saw someone on a horse galloping down the mountain. There was something odd about him, and we stopped working the horses and began to walk out towards him. He was just reaching us as he jumped from his horse, and between gasps of air he said:

"Aba! Aba![17] ... The black horse herd - a horse has gone wild and is running away. The other horses are following it. Kengesh and I just managed to stop the herd and we've left them in Kembel. I came straight to get you, and Kengesh is off chasing the wild horse – it has run far away.

He was always in a rush and exaggerated: if he ever heard about two men fighting somewhere he used to curse "damn, I wish I was there" and roll up his sleeves as if looking for a fight. I told him to be serious, calm down, take a deep breath and tell me what had happened, why the horse had run off, and where exactly the main herd was. I looked him straight in the eye and told him to tell me everything, with no messing about.

He started "Aba, we've been in Sandyk for a week. Buudaibek and Melis were looking after the mares that had given birth, and the others were counting the foals. They went only yesterday." Nasyr paused to take breath. His head was steaming with sweat and he used his whip to wipe away the sweat rolling down his brow.

---

[17] Translates as Brother, a common term used between direct relatives as well as good friends or colleagues

Around that place, every second or third year a wild mare used to show up. There was 'dancing grass' there, with poisonous roots. At least that's what people who knew a lot about poisons said. So the wild grey mare may have eaten the grass or its roots.

It suddenly all became clear in my mind.

I caught the fast stallion Karager, saddled up and jumped on him, leaving Nasyr to help milk the mares. I rode as fast as I could in the direction the wild mare had rode in.

My blessed horse, Karager, was fast and strong. Once I saddled him with 100 kilograms of flour, alongside myself, and rode him from the Chuy valley up through the steepest pass to Too Ashuu day and night. He never even raised a murmur.

I cared deeply about Karager, always feeding him well and on time. He was in excellent condition, neither skinny nor fat. When I rode to Bokso I let him pace himself and he ran as smooth as a flying eagle. When I reached Charyak I saw Kengesh, who was holding his horse. It was motionless, and clearly exhausted.

I ask him which way the wild mare had gone and then told him to go back home to Kichi Suusamyr where his horse could get some rest.

On the second day, I passed through a Kazakh village, and started asking about the lost horse. A woman, who was picking up cow pats, told me:

"Oh, dear man! Give me a reward for good news[18]. The horse you are looking for is tied up near the Kazakh House of Four." I had only twenty five roubles in my pocket and I duly gave it to her, and rode on as fast as I could.

My collar and sleeves were flapping until they nearly came off my shirt as I rode as fast as I could to the four yurts that I knew as the Kazakh House of Four. Nearby there was a luscious green marsh, ideal for grazing animals overnight. However, there was only one horse tied up there. As I searched around I could see little else except for one other mare which was grazing amongst a herd of sheep. It looked like their main animal was sheep.

The spaces between the yurts were dark and lifeless, so I walked to the biggest yurt and gave a shout:

---

[18] It is very common in Central Asia to give a reward, usually money, to people who have given good news

"Is anyone at home?"

The door to the yurt was already rolled up to its open position, and an old woman showed up, framed squarely in the entrance. She had an oversized coat over her shoulders which made her look deceptively skinny.

"Good health to you!" I shouted

"And to you, stranger."

"Do you have something to drink?" I asked, as I was very thirsty after the hard ride.

"But of course! Please come in," and she came forward to take my horse to paddock it.

I didn't give her my horse to tie up as she was a woman. We both, of course, understood that it was polite for her to offer but that I could not accept her offer. I tied my horse up to a pole, and went into the yurt.

"What can I offer you to drink? Horse milk or camel milk?"

"Horse milk, please."

The old woman put some honey and bread on a tray for me, before pulling the cloth off a large earthenware pot and ladling out a cup of her kymys. I tried a little bread and downed the kymys. It was a little sour, meaning it wasn't quite ready but I still downed it and slaked my thirst. I thanked her profusely for her kindness and hospitality and then went outside and got on my horse. As I expected, she followed me outside and I had a chance to explain why I was there and what I was looking for. She laughed:

"Good news, give me a reward."

I searched my pockets but I didn't have anything left, so I took off my waistcoat and gave it to her.

She folded the waistcoat over her arms and started: "We woke early, and close to where you and your horse are now standing was a grey mare. The poor horse was up to her knees in that marsh. My husband saw her and reckoned she had been eating 'dancing grass' and had run away from our Kyrgyz neighbours, especially after she kicked and bucked like crazy when we got her out of the swamp. We tied her to the pole, but she jumped around and snapped the stick, and then ran off as if she had been scared by a gunshot. My husband and all the others from the village have gone to try and catch her," she said, and pointed the other way from which I had come.

I don't even remember now if I whipped my Karager. The wind was blowing so fast that even my eyes were wet, but I still rode my horse as fast as I could.

As I reached Ketmen Tobo there was a spit of land where two separate rivers converged and I saw a mass of people waiting. I drove my horse towards the crowd, and as I passed the people I greeted them. As I neared the river bank an old man came forward and greeted me before looking me in the eye and telling me: "we have slaughtered your horse and we have been waiting for you to join us. We weren't sure if you would come but we're glad you are here."

I was aghast. My body went cold. Had they slaughtered my horse on purpose? What sort of people were they?

The old man continued, ignoring my expressions of disbelief. "Please don't be upset, dear friend. This morning when this mare arrived into our village we caught her and tied her up but she pulled out the pole where we had tied up a thousand horses before and ran off. We chased her and eventually found her here where she had impaled herself on an old tree stump on the way down to the river and pierced her stomach. We found her lying here in great distress and we slaughtered her as a kindness! After all, we are all Muslims. Are you going to take her away or are you going to leave her?"

"It is so hot, how could I take her with me! It would be far better to leave this meat for your village," and at that I made to whip my horse to leave.

"Hey, steady young man" the old man almost shouted in an angry voice. I turned around and looked at him. His white beard was shaking as his jaw quavered. As I brought my horse to a stop he said something to a young man who then set off towards their herd of horses grazing nearby. He led back a fine stallion and helped the old man onto its back. He then rode up beside me.

"We know you are upset for your mare but don't be. She will not go to waste where she lies: we will take the meat from her carcass and put it to good use feeding our people. We will give you a foal in her place."

It was a really pleasant surprise. Not just because they were giving me a foal but also because it reminded me that the Kazakhs were just like the Kyrgyz people. We shared one culture and they were essentially related to us like brothers and sisters with honest hearts. That's why I was really happy!

We went through the herd and the old man picked out a foal for me. We then took it back, tied it up outside his yurt and sat down for tea. As the samovar was being boiled I sat and drank kymys. The old man went down to the river and came back with water for the foal. I was sitting inside the yurt beside a pile of handmade blankets.

What a day it had been, riding my horse and searching for my mare. I was exhausted. It wasn't long before the blankets became too inviting and I took a nap. While I was asleep someone else arrived at the yurt, and the next thing I knew this person, who looked more like a beggar with his Asa Musa, was saying: "Wake up, it is not right that you are sleeping here when in Chychkan Valley at Kyzyl Oy your son has fallen from his horse and is badly injured and may die. The blue-white stallion is guarding him but you must get up and ride as fast as you can!"

The intensity in his voice made me believe him immediately and I got up straight away. I dashed out of the yurt with my white kalpak in one hand and my coat in the other, and was just about to put my shoes back on at the door when the old man returned. He looked at me questioningly and full of surprise.

"What is happening? My friend, you look so scared...please stay and pray with us," he said

"Old man! I have seen a ghost and he told me that my son is in grave danger. I have to go. Please do not be angry with me," I told him and jumped onto Karager.

The old man held my arm and gently asked me, "What is your name? That foal: who does it go to?" He was still holding my horse bridle.

"They should ask for me in the Suusamyr summer pasture, I am Uzagaaly. I'm the horse man with the long black beard who does the lights at night in the winter. Everybody knows me, at the big Kyrgyz village of Suusamyr: anyone could help you find me.

"Dear old man! Please give me your blessing!"

"Amin! Safe journey!" he said, and bowed his head to me

My dearest animal, Karager! He flew like a shooting star in the dark night. When the sun was just beginning to shine over the mountains I reached Kyzyl Oy.

At once I saw my son lying there. His legs were swollen and were turning dark blue. The fine animal, the blue-white stallion, was watching over him.

He had been guarding my son for some time. There was an empty grassless circle around him where he had been grazing. A further seven or eight paces out from the circle around my boy lay three or four dead jackals. It looked like they had been trying to prey on my boy, but the blue-white stallion had kicked them to death.

When I jumped from my horse my son opened his eyes and tried to whisper something. His lips were dry and he was mouthing the word "water", but no sound was coming out. I dashed over to the nearby caves and found a small spring bubbling with fresh water. I filled my silk-lined woolen kalpak with water and quickly returned. Although some of the water trickled out there was still plenty for my son. As he drank, he found his voice.

"Father, there is a bear here," he whispered. "While I was rounding up the horses it attacked us."

"Where is your friend Buudaibek?" I asked, fearing the answer.

"We were at Ilbirs spring on the top of the Chychkan Mountain, looking around this valley with our binoculars. We were watching Kengesh and Nasyr trying to round up all the horses in Altygan. One mare ran off and one of them went riding after her, while the other was droving the herd towards Kembel, and presumably from there back home."

"When Buudaibek saw the mare running away he said that it looked like that she had been eating 'dancing grass'. He told me that he would go to help to chase that mare, and that I should go and help round up the other horses and go to Bel Saz and try not to be late home. He took the snaring net and set off after the runaway mare."

"So why did you not go and take the herd home then?"

"When I got down to the valley I saw some horses beside that cave that you took the water from, and they were enjoying the green grass. I went to round them up ...." His voice trailed off.

"Oh, I see... and you met a bear? He was probably attracted by the wild sour leeks."

"I don't really know, I was singing a song, you know that one," and at that he started singing

"The fields are wild and beautiful
There is a dear screaming
I would like to go
But the dogs are barking
But my stomach is burning
If I don't go...I will be sad."

"OK, I understand, but the bear?" I managed to get out, though inside I felt my heart was being crushed and almost melting as my son sang the song.

He continued "And then it was suddenly dark behind me and something attacked my horse. I looked behind me and it was a huge bear! My horse screamed, then reared and I fell off onto my back. It felt like I had been hit by lightning. My eyes were blinded when I hit the ground and when I came back to my senses I couldn't see my horse at first. Then I did see it: my blue-white horse was bucking and biting five or six bears and keeping them at bay. He drove them all away and then came back to me and stood over me to protect me. For two days he didn't go away at all. He occasionally went over to the little hill, but neighed all the way there and back. Did you know that this horse has ears that light up like candles?" said my son. He tried to turn, but started moaning. "I can't feel my right leg or either of my arms at all. Yesterday, a fly annoyed me; it was buzzing around my face all day"

I wrapped my coat around my son and made him comfortable on a little mound as I set about saddling up the blue-white stallion. However Karager was keen to graze so, to stop him pulling his head down, I had to tie up his mouth. Once he was ready I led the blue-white horse to the mound and managed to lift my son onto him. I tied him onto the saddle, took the reins and mounted my own horse, and we headed off. I knew my son was in real pain but though he moaned in anguish he never once complained.

When we reached our home everything was calm and peaceful. There was no noise at all. When I opened the door to rush inside and get my wife I saw Turusbek the herbalist waiting for us. I was so pleased to see him.

"Oh my God! Thank you so much for being here," I almost shouted it out.

Turusbek had a long flowing white beard that gave him great gravitas. After we got our son inside and carefully laid him down the old herbalist started carefully massaging his head and neck. Then he pulled open his mouth and made him stick his tongue out. The herbal doctor studied my son's tongue intently. As he continued rubbing his body he asked question after question about both his physical ailments and what was on his mind that bothered him. My son spoke of how he had been lying in the sun, the place he had laid, and the part-hilly part-smooth rock outcrops that had surrounded him, how he had felt his legs break and how he had got his dark bruises. It all poured out. After the old man had massaged him down to his toes, he tapped all over my son's head. Lastly he massaged down his injured arms, causing my son's face to screw up in agony. As ended his examination, he carefully propped my son into a comfortable position, in which the dark coloured bruising on his torso and limbs was visible through the light coming from the door.

"Go and pick the Shyraljyn herb and boil it fast in a clean and deep pot," he directed my wife, and then turned back to study the injuries.

After she had gone outside, he asked Kengesh and Nasyr to hold him up and he put a piece of wood down one side of his body from his armpit to his toes, and tied this to his torso and leg to act as a splint. My son's face winced in pain but he never once cried out. As they laid him back down the old man was massaging his shoulders above his injured arms, and started telling a funny story. As the story went on, I saw my son visibly relax. Then all of a sudden the herbal doctor's hand slipped down to the boy's left wrist and he pulled the arm so fast that my boy didn't know what was coming. The scream was deafening before he slumped into unconsciousness. Turusbek didn't pay the slightest attention, and duly went about working the arm until every joint clicked back into place and the arm looked normal again, albeit still bruised around the joints. He then pulled and straightened the joints on the other arm in a similar manner. To finish off the treatment of the arms, he applied a gentle massage, and as he was doing this my boy regained consciousness.

Smiling, Turusbek went outside to where my wife had just returned and started boiling the Shyraljyn. "Please, it is now time to take it inside the house. Pass it through a clean sieve into a clean pot, and before it cools pour it into the bath." At that he went back inside.

He looked at me with his sharp eyes, raised his head and told me: "find a young goat that has only eaten Ermen[19]."

I didn't have any such goat but I knew that my friend Amankul in a nearby jailoo would have such a beast, so I rode there quickly on my blue-white stallion. As I rode back into our compound, the goat was bleating loudly as I held it over the front of my saddle. Turusbek was helping my son bathe in the boiled Shyraljyn water. At the same time he was encouraging him to drink cow's milk laced with herbs from a spoon. The mixture looked less than inviting and it was little wonder that he initially refused to drink it. However Turusbek was extremely patient and he got it down him, even though this was followed by consummate gagging and coughing. As the bathing continued we slaughtered the goat and skinned it. After my son was lifted out of his bath, we applied the fresh and warm skin to his bloated and bruised leg. He winced with pain and we had to hold him down with his good leg and his two bandaged arms. As Turusbek started to sew up the goat skin, he eventually began to relax again.

Turusbek asked me to count the broken bones and how they recovered until he had finished sewing the goat skin and holding tight, he said with a smile. Thereafter he worked the goat skin into a slim and comfortable strapping for the broken leg. As he was stitching it up, he stopped frequently, whispering something and biting his lips. Often he pretended he was stitching when he was actually massaging my son's legs. This continued for many hours well into the evening. Every time I counted the broken bones bulging from the leg there appeared to be one less: who knows how every break became normal again and the swelling and bruises disappeared. The upper half of the skin was never stitched and, as the leg looked more and more normal, he eased the stitches out, removing the skin, replacing it with a white material compress of his own prepared Shak Shak herb, and carefully bandaging the boy's leg. To finish he rolled a hand-made woolen carpet around the leg, and put pillows under and over it.

The goats' intestine had been boiled, and he poured out one cup of stock to which he added one spoon of the medicinal herb Shybak. After it was infused, and while it was still warm, he held my son's head in his arm and tried to feed him. He was

---

[19] Another herb used for medicinal purposes

in pain and was refusing to drink, and only Turusbek's insistence got him to drink it all. As the last of the herbal stock drained from the cup into his system, his face became pink and alive. After a brief sweat he fell fast asleep!

It was only after all the drama that we asked ourselves the questions. Had Turusbek, the herbal doctor, arrived at our house for a specific reason? He had said he was looking for new herbs to add to his medicinal collection. He had mentioned a man from Andijan called Malik, who had supposedly been preparing these since early spring and was apparently expecting him. He had collected two herbs, Ermen and Kokomeren, which are both used for medicinal purposes when dried.

"Today I was supposed to go Balykty and tomorrow I was supposed to carry on, that's why I left my house so early," said the herbal doctor. His beard was as white as a swan's down. He had a wide forehead, which gave his words weight when he spoke. His shadow made him look a very strong man. He was said to be about a hundred years old, yet was fit enough to hunt like a young man and climb in the mountains.

We had all heard a lot about him. His skills with herbs were famous not only in Suusamyr and Jumgal, but also as far away as Ketmen Tobo, the Fergana valley, Andijan, Talas, Jambyl and Chuy.

People spoke of him as a legend. He had reportedly drunk 'holy water' from the very highest of the mountains, which only Kaibergen the fabled Mother of the Mountain Goats could reach. Whether or not this was true, his face looked so very alive and young.

Turusbek continued: "Now, the water of the Koko Meren River is very wild and the bridge nearby may have been wiped away by its power. That's why I came the longer way, via the bridge from Toskok to Balykty. On that bridge I met a beggar.

"I was so happy, because beggars can count the stars, and are very knowledgeable doctors as well. They know which herbs are ready to collect, which star is shining brightest, and what kinds of illness the herbs will help to cure. They know this like the backs of their hands.

"I greeted him, and asked him some questions which were very important to me. The beggar told me that in the Sandyk area there was a horseman called

Uzagaaly. His son had fallen from a horse, broken his arm and leg, and lain two days in a field. His father was taking him home and would be sending someone to ask me to go and help them. I turned around straight away and came here to your home. When I arrived everything seemed so calm here and there was no sign of anyone in need. I thought, "Oh, poor beggar, looks like he lost his mind. I was about to drink a cup of kymys when you arrived with your injured son." Turusbek looked at me very suspiciously "Looks like he met you first?"

I did not know what to say! It looked like when I was asleep in our Kazakh friend's house, a ghost appeared who sent the herbal doctor here. I thought he was the Holy Aleikumsalam himself. I prayed inside for forgiveness for my lie.

"Yes, he met me at Mumio Cliff. But how did he manage to get down faster than me without a horse? I answered with a deep breath.

"Of course it could be that the 'beggar' is not an ordinary person. Perhaps he is a divine being," said Turusbek, touching his white beard.

"Let's have something to eat, if the food is ready. We will dine early and get to sleep. I have to get up very early and collect some very important herbs from my house so I can help this little hero. I am not going to Andijan then!" said Turusbek.

While we were eating, Buudaibek arrived, the stupid man who had left my son alone in the pasture.

He looked like a sparrow with his thin face, big mouth and small eyes. That's all you saw when you looked at him. Even the robe he was holding had been given by me as a reward for good news last year. He was holding the foal which had come over from our Kazakh friends.

He was about forty years old and was here instead of Seyit, who had fallen from his horse in Sasyk Bulak and later lost his leg in hospital: he was a real horseman. If only he had been there instead.

Buudaibek was quite the opposite. In that selfish age, his main purpose in life was to take care of himself, and he did a great job of that. All he desired was a clean river and grass to grow for his horses. He was certainly a strange young fellow: I almost called him a comedian because of his strange attitude.

"Ah...Markabay the Kazakh man sent you this, brother" he said, as he held the foal, looking at it and me together. His thick eyebrows made him look like a frog, about to leap. He didn't even said "hello" to any of us, which just illustrated his bad manners.

I mocked him straight away. "Hey, young magician, you did a great job, a really big thing. Well, now add this foal to the herd in Kym Bel. While the herd is accepting him, do not walk away for three days and nights," I said. When a new horse is put into a herd, we need to watch to make sure that it is going to be accepted by the other horses. If not, there is usually a sad ending.

"OK brother," he said, and he started to walk with his horse, which walked like an old clip-clop. He then mounted it.

"For goodness sake, old man, you should at least offer a cup of kymys," said my wife, who went outside after him.

He had heard and turned his horse's head back "All right, my brother, I will have a cup of kymys," he said, and jumped down from his horse.

I was smiling, but inside I was angry and almost ready to shoot the scabby dog.

"Be quiet. After you add this foal to the main herd, you will drink kymys somewhere: but not in my house."

"OK, my brother. It will be as you say. I will do that." He almost crawled back onto his big horse, and we only saw his shoulders as he held his head in shame before mounting his horse, taking the foal over his saddle and riding off.

Turusbek, who was watching this, smiled. "Poor man, why are you punishing him so hard?"

"It is his entire fault." I couldn't hide my anger. "You are lucky that you don't have to live with what he does."

If he had only done what I told him to do, nothing would have happened. If only he knew how to chase away an animal. He does not know the poisons of the Earth. It isn't as if he had never heard of wild tigers and bears in the Chychkan cliff area! How could he leave my six-year-old boy in that wild, dangerous place, like a little crow? If he had really wanted to chase a crazy mare, he should have made everything safe and then chosen the best and fastest stallion instead of his hungry and slow old horse. He didn't even change his riding horse in the spring - if you gave that old nag a strong tug on its eyelash it would fall over. How was he ever going to chase a young, fast and crazy running mare? He just thought but never gave it any real consideration: he is just utterly mad. Shame on him for thinking he was a real horseman with extensive knowledge of horses. His conscience should not be clear.

"He has an honest heart and when he saw the accident he did not think about anything other than trying to help you, that's why he was in a hurry," said Turusbek with a smile.

The next day Turusbek left early in the morning, and then came back the same afternoon with his medicinal herbs. He immediately started his treatment.

Very carefully he boiled up some dried herbs in a kazan. First he boiled Ermen, and then he added two bucketfuls of water and boiled it up a couple of times. Each time he took the kazan off the fire to cool down a little on the stone hearth we call a kemege. After this, he added two Ak Kodol leaves and three Kokomeren roots, and left it all to infuse.

When it had cooled down he reached for the left over muslin from cream straining that lay near the kazan, and he sieved the mixture through the clean white material. He pulled something out of his pocket which was rolled up in tin foil, a crushed dried flower. He sprinkled some of the crushed flower on top.

My curiosity kicked in "What is that herb, Aksakal?" I asked the herbalist.

"This is the 'Soul of the Mountains', a most precious flower. This is Edelweiss. Last year I picked it when I was hunting wild goats at Oi Kayng."

"What is it for, Aksakal? How will this and all the other herbs help a broken leg?"

Turusbek stared at me "Uzagaaly, how old are you?"

Nobody had ever asked me that question before in my life. How old was I? I wasn't sure what to say so I simply said "I am in my sixty-fourth year," and tried to smile.

"You have passed Jesus' age. Now it is time to stop being stupid," he replied with some sadness. "Look, there is only thirty years' difference between us, and yet you ask me questions which my son's grandchild would not ask. A broken bone is easy to cure fast. Normally I would only give mumue[20] which would heal him when mixed with conifers and given ten times. This case is different. I am worried about his future, as his injures could last a long time and may result in incurable black bones[21].

"Black bones is something mostly contracted by animals. Wild goats and domestic animals generally contract it with foot and mouth disease. I suspect that the place in the field where the boy fell and lay for almost two days surrounded by grasses was where ill animals had died from the disease a long time ago. This disease is still very much alive there and wants to spread, and has badly affected the boy's broken leg. Usually after suffering this disease the animals should be burned and destroyed completely, not just buried, or the chances are that it will return through the grass and the disease will spread again.

"That's what I am worried about. Your heart makes you blind or you would see how dangerous this case really is. Look at this swelling," and at that he waved his hand towards an ugly lump on my son's leg before stating: "you just do not understand." Then he continued...

"Our ancestors said that for centuries Kyrgyz have used seven different herbs to treat black bones. They were Edelweiss, Ermen, Ak Kodol, Shyraljyn, Kokomeren, Shybak and Uu korgoshun.

"Some herbal doctors also use Barpy, a herb you will also hear mentioned from time to time. I rarely use it myself because it is very hard to find, especially growing on the sunny side of the mountains. I did find some Barpy* on the shady side, but I used it very sparingly to cure illnesses."

It really was something I knew little about and I felt so ashamed I was now looking down.

Turushek then stopped speaking and with a different voice told me "Uzagaaly... You can always find a new animal but you cannot always find a new son, can you! Please slaughter a fat mare now. Even if you have to sell your hat to get such an animal! We need some fresh and warm horse fat. That is the first thing. Second, please crush some Uu korgoshun from my bag. I dug up these roots this past winter.

---

[20] *White mouse droppings used for medicinal purposes, still used today in lotion for flu*
[21] *Bone cancer*

79

All the other herbs will help clear up the inside swelling, while the outside swelling will be cleared up with Uu korgoshun.

"Mai Jaryl village is surrounded with Uu korgoshun. Late this autumn or after the first snowfall please go to the swamp and dig a lot of Uu korgoshun. I may need it in the future. Do not dig everything up, just the plants which are already sprouting again above the ground: only their roots are useful."

After lecturing me, Turusbek turned back to his kazan and checked the boiled herbs with his finger. He raised my little boy's head up. "You should drink at least half of this." He almost begged him. My boy drank everything with a wrinkled-up face. Turusbek encouraged him "Good boy… What a real man you are! I have helped cure a lot of heroes. They used to cry so much that even God heard their voices. You are just a little boy, yet you do not cry at all. You are a very patient young man. It looks like your father doesn't know about anything except his horses and although he spends all his time and energy with them you are still such a strong character that you do not suffer from lack of attention. You are a brave hero indeed!

"Now, one more time, you need to be very patient. You will thank me for the rest of your life. I will now give you Uu korgoshun instead of the Shak Shak I gave you before.

Can you see how this swelling is rising to the top of your leg? If it migrates to your stomach you may well lose your leg. That's why we have to try and suck it back with this new herb, Uu korgoshyn. This one will affect your bone's injured marrow and stop the swelling. Otherwise your leg will turn to black bone…"

"Grandfather, what is this illness? Is it bad?"

"It is better that you don't know the illness. Better that you don't even think about it, agreed?"

My son nodded.

"Well done! You really are brave. Looks like you are heir of our legendary hero Manas! If I cure you and make you like a new young stallion, what will you give me back as a present?"

"I will give you a horse, and a new chapan!" said my son. Turusbek was very surprised.

"Gosh, you are very generous! You talk like a grown-up! "

I could see Turusbek considering his reply so as to impart more of his wisdom from his near one hundred years of age. He started: "Sometimes, my brave hero, you should temper your generosity. Some people's ears would quickly prick up and they would take everything they could from you, whether they deserved it or not!"

Not for the first time he glanced over at me with a little anger and continued with his lecture "Uzagaaly, he is growing as a person with a very honest heart and whilst that is good in many respects you must also teach him that there are times when he must exercise caution. My boy, don't always reveal your generosity to people, particularly when you have just met them. Learn to listen and appreciate the situation."

I felt I had to explain myself: "It is not my fault dear Aksakal Turusbek." I did not know what to say but stammered on "He is always with other children, day and night, playing in the field…"

"Stop there. You should spend more time with him and teach him some of your worldly wisdom so he can behave like you. You let him spend time with spoiled young kids, shame on you. A young boy's feelings are very strong, what he sees he repeats, and what he hears he says. This kind of thing could turn very ugly too, you know," said Turusbek. I would have been offended to have been lectured like this by others, but Turusbek had such stature I felt myself openly accepting the criticism.

Turusbek then quietly got on with changing the bandages. Holding his legs high up, he half unwrapped the Shak Shak bandages and emptied out the herb, before replacing it with the prepared Uu korgoshun, which he had crushed and added to boiling water. Once in place, and with the bandages tightly wrapped again, he slowly rubbed the injured legs through the herb-laden bandage.

"Well, my hero, you should calm down and sleep. You will be a good patient even if it is painful. You are going to be a good patient, aren't you? Please say you are!"

"I will, Grandfather!"

"You should say it three times!" said Turusbek following the old superstition of saying important phrases three times.

"I will Grandfather! I will Grandfather! I will Grandfather!"

"Well done! You are really Manas' heir, aren't you? Now you had better keep your word. It is our hero's motto that if he promises to do something he will do it even if it is really hard. I think you are a hero."

Looking at them, my son truly seemed like a hero. I really valued now how Turusbek had inspired my son with his words.

We drank kymys and went outside. The sun was setting and it was getting dark. About half the herd which had been milked had now returned to the jailoo and were contentedly to grazing. The milking of the remaining half was well underway. Turusbek looked at his black mare and asked me, "Do you have a fast horse, Uzagaaly?"

"Yes, I have my Karager."

"Not that one, the poor animal looks very tired, and needs to get his strength up. If he doesn't he may not be here to eat grass tomorrow morning. Catch a snake, cut six inches off his head and six from his tail, add some wheat and feed it to him. He is a very fine animal: do not lose him."

"What do you need a fast horse for, Aksakal?"

"I need one: not just a fast horse but one with a pure and precious pedigree!"

"Oh, yes, I have that kind of horse. A blue-white stallion!"

"Then please fetch him for me and help me saddle him."

"No problem, Aksakal."

"After the sun sets your son's temperature will go up. He will struggle to breathe. Let him sniff the crushed wheat often. Do not, though, give him any water. Even if he begs and cries, do not listen to him. I am going to ride your blue-white stallion and make him sweat three times. When the stars are full in the sky I shall be back. If the boy survives tonight he is going to be all right. In the early morning you should have a mare ready to slaughter. "

When Turusbek returned to our home, God help us, my boy was suffering. He was sweating badly and squeezing his fist at the times he came back to reality to overcome the discomfort.

"I am going to be a good patient, Grandfather," he repeated over and over again.

Turusbek gave an order to all of us. "Take the boy, wrap him in a shyrdak[22] and carefully take him outside. Be careful with his broken leg."

The sky was full of stars like a flowery garden when we took my son outside. The blue-white stallion was breathing deeply and was damp with sweat. Turusbek lifted my son towards the stallion's neck. He raised his head higher up until his nose was close to the horse's sweating flanks. The boy, who was fighting for his life, was breathing slowly and he moved his head closer, taking in the smell of the horse. After a while he opened his eyes and saw Turusbek in front of him, holding the stallion's mane to let the vapours escape.

He smiled finally and asked, "Was I a good patient, Grandfather? "

"Yes, well done! You truly are a hero. You did not ask for your mother or father even once. The danger is now over. You should breathe the blue-white stallion's sweat in deeply. This is very important for your life."

Only when the stars started disappearing did my son fall into a smooth and peaceful sleep.

Turusbek announced "Well! Well! God has blessed him. The boy has survived. He will be fine now! Please take him back inside very carefully: he needs to rest. And do not move his broken leg! "

Before the sun rose Turusbek slaughtered the large mare I had brought. He peeled off the inside fat and put it to one side to cool. From his pocket he again produced the tin foil that contained the crushed Soul of the Mountain, and he sprinkled some over the smooth fat.

---

[22] Traditional felted rug

He went inside the house and woke my sleeping son. He gave him the fresh smooth fat to eat, and he duly ate it all before going straight back to sleep. I didn't even really notice that he was eating raw horse fat.

As the morning wore on, Turusbek took some Shak Shak and boiled it in a kazan. Then he added three herbs: Ermen, Ak Kodol and Shyraljyn. After boiling he let the liquid cool a little before pouring it into a cup. While it was still warm he washed the boy's legs. He repeated this process throughout the day. In the evening, before bed time, he wrapped up the leg with Uu-korgoshun. After one month, my boy recovered and it was only when Turusbek was sure that boy was on the way to full recovery that he returned to his own home.

As he set off on his journey home my wife went to him. "Father, your collar should always be white and your clothes should be new," said my wife, and gave him handmade clothes that she had sewed herself.

Turusbek was so glad that he blessed her to show his appreciation.

For my part I wanted to give Turusbek a horse. "Aksakal, please ride this! I got this horse as a reward for looking after my herd so well in the winter. It should be yours!

"I do not want this treasure. Any man who is born should do good things because they can and without any regrets. My father, who passed away a long time ago, used to tell me this. Oh, he was such a talented herbal doctor. The only people he could not cure were the dead! Everyone else he could cure and he did. I was so lucky and pleased to help people to recover as my father taught me. I helped all of them who were ill, or had bone cancer. But, in the case of your son, I made sure that his broken bones would not lead to gangrene. I haven't lived a hundred years for nothing. So, now I have an idea. Please, send me your boy when spring arrives. In three years I will teach him how to collect the herbs and all their secrets and maybe in the future he will be a talented herbal doctor too. That will give you something to deeply respect as well as (instead of) your horses." The Aksakal put his hand on my son's shoulder "He is stubborn, with fire in his heart. He keeps his word. He has the character of a strong man and will grow up with a good personality."

He continued: "My father always used to tell me that I was shy and slow but I would become someone. He was a good man and a wise man, it seems, as he could predict the future. Later in my life it was really my own fault for I was too late to teach my own children. They are no use now. They only know how to drink vodka. It is so frustrating. This gift should not die with me, it should stay with humanity." The Aksakal then looked at my wife "this daughter-in-law does not seem interested in this!"

My wife turned around and said very quietly "Father, he will soon be seven and we want him to go to school"

"School! "retorted Turusbek "I had no formal education and didn't even know the alphabet. But look at me, I am still quite a knowledgeable herbal doctor and have managed to look after myself all my life. He could go to school when he turns ten."

"It would be too late for him, father"

"It is never too late. At this age he would be able to remember all about herbs. What he will learn after he has graduated from school?" said Turusbek, with a furrowed brow.

I didn't know what to say to this very old and respectable man. It wasn't clear what to do. He was almost begging us, so I asked my son: "Would you like to be like this Grandfather, a herbal doctor?"

"Yes," my son replied without hesitation.

"Then, in spring, when Grandfather comes to take you away, you will not cry?"

"I have never cried in my life!" said my son, proudly. "If Grandfather gave me permission to ride my horse, I could even go today!"

"Well done. You are going to be someone. Better I talk with you directly instead of these two who look after you," said the old man. He was very happy. "God bless you, my son. Live a very long life," and at that he bent down to hug him and kiss his forehead.

"You cannot really ride just now. Don't worry, when the winter is over, you will not feel like your bones were broken. I will come in the spring to collect you. Deal?"

In order to seal the deal, my son and Turusbek shook each other's small fingers. Then they chewed hay and drank some water.

I personally accompanied Turusbek back to his house. We then ate with his grandson, Janysh. Turusbek appeared to live alone in his two room house, as his wife had passed away almost twenty years ago. In talking I learned that he spent his time making herbal medicines, playing his komuz[23] and sometimes going hunting.

I was offered young fresh lamb to eat, and we relaxed and talked. The next day I was ready to ride my horse home. Before mounting, Turusbek gave me his final instructions for my boy "When the weather gets colder and winter is approaching, rub badger's fat very lightly onto his leg, shoulder and his elbow. This will stop the cold getting to his bones. Add dried yoghurt to lamb stock to help his bones develop well. They are very soft now but this will make them strong. Sew some goatskin trousers for him to wear in the winter. Don't give him old shoes with smooth shoes or let him go skating. And finally, don't let him ride a horse until spring."

He told me all this with great pleasure. As I left his home I felt deep respect for his almost century of healing, and how passionate he was about it. You could almost feel his kindness.

Time passed…

Then, before the New Year, Turusbek fell very ill with flu. Winter was really harsh in the area and I heard he couldn't even get out of bed.

I decided we should visit him and my son and I wrapped ourselves up in our sheepskin handmade warm coats: my son's was black and mine was red, (I used to wear it when looking after horses on cold nights). I rode my Karager with my son at my back to visit him and enquire after his health. When we reached his house the poor old man obviously wasn't well.

His sons were already growing their own beards, as symbols of their age and their possible imminent elevation up the family tree. They were fussing round the old man, taking care of him and bustling in and out of the house.

He was very happy to see us: his eyes lit up and he smiled. After greeting us, he

---

[23] *A traditional stringed instrument*

nodded to his eldest son who was nearly fifty years old and had a black beard. The son stood up, took his komuz in his hand and started playing.

"I thought I was waiting for someone before passing away, but I could not think who," said the old man, with a squeaky voice that sounded like a komuz being played, and a cheeky smile on his face.

"It has been annoying me that I could not remember who was supposed to come, but you arrived just in time, my little child." His voice quavered a little, and I understood he was talking to my son. "Could you show me your leg, please?"

Melis left my side, went over to him and took off his handmade woollen shoes. He pulled up one side of his goatskin trousers, and showed his leg to the old man. Turusbek put out his arm and gently massaged the leg. He held his fingers like he was measuring a pulse and said: "Now you can stop spreading badger fat." Then he took his hand back slowly: "now show me your shoulder "

My son took off his shirt quickly and stood before Turusbeck.

Turusbeck shouted for his grandson: "Janysh! Where is Janysh, that rotten grandson of mine? He is always doing something when I need him here."

"He went to feed and water the horses," said Janysh's wife.

"Call him please. Tell him to come quickly as I need his help now," said the old man in a deep grumpy voice with his eyebrows pulled together. His eldest son was playing his komuz very loudly now. I didn't know the tune but I imagined someone riding up to the house on a fast horse.

A horse did indeed arrive at the house and Janysh's wife went outside.

Just outside I heard an angry voice, presumably that of another of Turusbek's sons. "I've told everyone a hundred times to tie the horses up further away from my house, not here. How many times do I have to say it? My tongue will soon grow longer giving all these instructions over and over again"

As the young man came in to the house it was obvious this was Janysh, a young man full of life with a cheeky grin. The woman identified as his wife was whispering something in his ear, obviously letting him know what he was walking into. Janysh walked over quickly and stood respectfully in front of his grandfather.

"Janysh! Hold this boy's left shoulder very tightly: now we will see how strong you are!"

At first he clearly didn't understand what his Grandfather wanted of him, and then as it dawned upon him he went over and squeezed my son's shoulder hard with his sturdy arms. Melis sat down, but did not utter a single sound.

"Let him go, you bear!" said the old man, his eyes suddenly bright as he shifted into his vocational mode. "Now hold his right elbow"

This time the young man wasn't so sure, and he looked at his grandfather when he squeezed boy's elbow. My son screamed and stood up, frozen to the spot in pain. The old man raised his head from his pillow.

"Damn. That's annoying!"

"It seems that when I was trying to put back the dislocated bones it didn't work well and a hernia formed. You will have to stop spreading badger fat: it seems a virus in the bones has turned the inside septic. Next it will fester inside the bones, and the infection may spread to the blood and the whole body. Why did you not look after him during this cold bloody winter?"

He was very angry but mainly talking and arguing with himself. "You will have to take him to Frunze at least now to see a doctor. However even if you take him there they will say it is a minor injury, though that diagnosis would be wrong. They will then just put a plaster cast on it. I've heard of them doing that many times, and then when they take the cast off thinking that the arm will be cured they find that it isn't and that the patient is now disabled. That's why you shouldn't go there, as nothing will cure it better than letting it heal naturally – my way, as I am fond of saying, which is so much better and more effective."

That animal of a grandson has no sense. God gave him physical strength and it looks like he squeezed Melis's elbow so hard that it is going to flare up and really hurt him for a week or so. You must start treating him right away. From today put Uu korgoshyn on his arm: it will help the poison gather. After the poison has burst out, wash the arm twice a day with a mixture of clean water and manganese.

The herb Shyraljyn would be much better, but I have no idea where you might find it, and anyhow you don't know how to use it. The inside of the bone is warm, and it will dry out nicely and get better. You need to find the green and blue herb Uu korgoshun which has just started growing at this time of year. Pull the white root out and put a needle and cotton thread through it, then put it inside the wound. Start by putting it in for just a few minutes, but later leave it in for longer. The thread will allow you to pull it out. When the pus is such that it does not bother him anymore, the boy's mouth will start spluttering. You should stop right then.

"When he starts spluttering give him cow's milk quite often. If you don't he could be poisoned and die. The wound will take a long time to heal because the flesh needs to grow back alongside the bone. After the wound is fully recovered you should sometimes put Uu Korgoshun on it. When spring is arriving, some birds will be flying back to this area: a little bird with blue feathers will peck for something in front of your house.

Those birds will disappear straight after the snow melts. Be very careful and catch a Kegaly bird. Break its neck, ensure it is fully plucked and then boil it. Give the stock to your son and make sure none of it is wasted. It is very important to make his bones strong, and that bird stock is the answer," said the old man.

He stopped talking for a while. After a few minutes his head moved as if to speak but he couldn't. He looked at his youngest son and then at Melis as if he wanted to speak, but his head only slumped forward onto the pillow and a thin trail of grey smoke came out of his mouth. That was his last breath or his untold sadness.

Nobody cried. The old man's eldest son played his komuz as they put up a yurt and took his body into it. It was only as they left the body, when the curtains were pulled to and the komuz playing ceased that Janysh wrapped his arms around himself and gave a loud cry.

We paid our respects to the old man in traditional Kyrgyz style by staying, praying and receiving guests for the three days after he passed away. After that my son and I wanted to go home and we asked permission from the new head of the household.

Turusbeks eldest son had told us that Janysh his eldest son was now in charge of everything. That had been his father Turusbeks last request. Turusbek had told them all to follow Janyshs orders. He had declared this in front of everyone, making sure it was well witnessed. Now what was Janysh going to say to us?"

"Please come into the house. Have a cup of tea. I have something which belongs to you," said Janysh, and he looked around. He shouted to a boy who was playing outside far away, "Hey! Could you find me the Shopocholick please?"

As we were drinking our tea, someone arrived at the front door. He was tall, and when he came in the house he gave off a strong stench of alcohol. He didn't join us for tea, but sat down on a little chair near the corner. Janysh did not like his uncle, he was a second son and Janysh thought of him as spoilt; he looked at him with disdain and turned to me.

"Before my grandfather died he said that someone would come whom he was expecting. He asked that even as we put up a yurt for him after he passed away that we shouldn't cry but just have the komuz played as he taught his eldest son. Janysh continued: "you have seen that we have done everything he wished."

He then turned and unleashed a tirade at his uncle: "He never had time to wipe the sweat from his forehead: his two arms were busy working so hard all his life to look after the family. Please, do not spare any expenses now that he is gone: wash his body, wrap him in white cotton, and ride on a horse, before burying him. He was born from the soil and is going back to soil. He was a hundred years old, celebrate it! Yes, we should celebrate it with others as much as we can but we should not drink ourselves into a stupor!"

Turning back to me he said "You have seen, along with the other village people, that his will was done. Now we must deal with what he left me, his youngest grandson, to deal with. Now is the time to make his wish come true!"

"Please say something, my uncle." He looked at his drunken uncle, who was sitting in the corner of the house.

He stared back into mid-space somewhere between Janysh and me. "What has it to do with these people?" He then proceeded to burp, releasing a strong and pungent smell of alcohol.

Janysh looked at his uncle with total surprise:

"What do you mean? Grandfather told us that after he passed away the person who came last to the house while he was still alive was to be given his herbs, his hunting gear and his staff"

"Yes of course!" he laughed, then coughed and burped "Of course! The last one who entered, that is what he said! They weren't the last ones who entered the door before father passed away. You were the last one: you had been feeding and watering the horses. Hadn't you!"

It was as if he was deliberately trying to make everyone in the house angry.

"Do you know what you are saying, you drunkard! Janysh did not know what else to say. He stood up. "Grandfather didn't want to give it to me: he asked me to look after the farm."

"You little shit, are you pointing at me, eh?" said the drunk uncle whilst he continued his hiccups. He managed to stand up. "I will show you, pointing at me… That was given to me, by my father. I will give it to the last man who entered the door. They are very precious things, why should I give them to the strangers who came in before you?

"Stop it!" Janysh screamed: "Just shut up, you stupid arse. I am now responsible for what goes on in this house. That means I am the owner. These people are my guests. I will not let you harm my guests."

"Look at him… Powerful man! Turusbek's authority now belongs to all his sons and grandsons and that means me as well." He clapped his chest and continued his rant. "You are not the man that my grandfather was" and he pointed out to where Janysh's grandfather lay "You are the stupid son of that man who was unlawfully married, you are his piss!"

"What?" Janysh punched his drunken brother, who fell into the corner where the bread was stored. His mouth and nose were bleeding. As he staggered back up he took up the poker for the fire which was lying in the corner.

"I will fry and eat your kidneys!" He moved to attack Janysh. Janysh's wife screamed. I don't know how but I got between them – Janysh and his drunken uncle but the drunken uncle then focused directly on me. He lunged at me screaming "It's your fault, you stupid bear!"

He struck my chest with the sharp end of the poker. I was in agony, and that was the last I remember from that day.

The next day, I woke up at the farm hospital. It looked like the poker had pierced the left side of my chest. I was in hospital convalescing for more than a month.

When I got back to my house, my son's arm was terribly red and swollen, and his voice was a whisper only God could have heard. My poor boy, he had suffered a lot.

I did everything that Turusbek the herbal doctor had wished at his last. I followed his orders exactly and finally, nearly half a year later, my son recovered.

Thank God for Turusbek Aksakal, rest in peace, Thank God for his soul…

It was very calm and quiet. My Father looked at the moon which had now nearly set, and then looked at me. "That's all, my dear son! You are only walking today because of the care Turusbek gave you. It is true that Monks and Beggars are of the same kin, and we should give thanks to God for them and never hinder their paths.

"And what happened to that old man's present for you, the one you describe as God's creature?" asked our current Beggar, who was lying between us, listening intently to my Fathers story.

"After Janysh took me to the farm centre hospital, where the doctors kept me for a month, he knew he would have to find a way to return Melis to my home. As he searched for a horseman to take Melis, he left his house on two or three occasions and his brother, the drunken madman, kept hovering around the place where his father's staff was lying. It was only after it suddenly disappeared on his return to the house that his brother confessed that, although he knew it was a very precious thing, he reckoned it would be better for it to depart with Turusbek rather than with a stranger. So he burned it rather than let it go with the person whom Turusbek had chosen for it. It was a really difficult situation and he knew he had done wrong, and eventually he turned himself in to the police. What a damned annoying jealous man: he burned the staff which had belonged to his Grandfather… utter madness…

I raised myself a little bit and after many years of wondering I now felt I had to ask a question that had been bothering me for years; now I was ready to ask:

"Why did Janysh's uncle call him 'illegitimate piece of piss do you know the answer to that?

My father continued his story...

I learned later ..... It was all to do with the time when people came back from exile, after the October Revolution. Janysh's father was only a thirteen year old boy. He had started riding horses in his early years and also played the komus very well. In his village there was a young beautiful girl, the daughter of a rich man. As a teenage boy full of courage and passion he went to her house regularly to propose to her, but her father sent him away and reprimanded him badly, telling him so many rotten things: that his father was a useless herbal doctor only good for picking grasses; that he was young, useless and naïve; and lots of other unkind things. However the suitor had fire in his heart: he was very brave with very strong feelings, and these were only strengthened by the numerous scoldings

For one week he rested his best horse. Then one day before sunset, he took the horse, put his sword in his belt, took his father's black 'Barang' gun which was normally left in the fireplace, and walked down to his beloved's village.

He sneaked up to the girl's bedroom window. "Ak Zyinat!" he called, and she came to the window "your father is just human: it is only your mother who gives you oxygen for life. We need to run away from here to find our paradise or it will turn into your hell. Everyone has freedom of choice and we should take our chance for happiness! Your father is famous for his huge flock of sheep which could feed the whole village for an entire winter but we both know he would never do that as he has a heart of stone. Maybe you will find a better man than me, but you are the most precious thing in the whole wide world for me. If you love me, let's leave your father's 'paradise' and set off on our own life journey.

Zyinat, young and beautiful, jumped down from the window and went to him. She stood in front of him, gazed up with her green eyes(she was only sixteen), and put her arms around his neck "Oh, my young hero, as soon as I heard that you were resting your horse, I collected enough food for the two of us and my belongings. But we only have one horse, how could he possibly carry both of us and our possessions." Tears rolled down her cheeks.

The young man replied "Take only what you really need for yourself: leave everything else."

Zyinat undid her package and tossed various items back in through the window, keeping only what could be tied up in a small white sheet. She spread her little korpocho[24] onto the back of the horse that had been standing patiently and jumped on. She rode the horse in the same style as a young boy.

Before setting off he walked slowly back to the house and banged loudly on the door. Once he heard a noise behind it he shouted: "Rich man, I am not kidnapping your daughter, that's what I came to say, bless your daughter and me. Don't send anyone to chase us or you will be responsible for someone getting injured. Goodbye!" At that he turned, ran and jumped onto the back of his horse behind Zyinat. He took the reins from her, goaded the horse into a full gallop and headed out the village towards Joo Jyrok.

The rich man was livid. He called every man in the village and challenged them to catch the couple, but as they went to fetch their horses they found the young man was not as useless as he had been told. The empty horse paddocks and trail of hoof marks leading away towards the mountains suggested he had been busy all night.

Once the horses had been corralled from the mountain, the pursuing party got under way, only to find as they reached the villages along the Joo Jyrok route. That was time when kymys had fermented well, and that no-one had seen the young couple.

A good half day ahead of the main search party, the young couple reached Kara Boor, a small village straddling six main routes. The young man banged his black "barang" gun-one more time, around and the whole village heard it. Then he spurred his horse on and they sped off again.

That evening, when the pursuing party finally reached the village, they saw the sword stuck in the centre of the Kara Boor crossroads and they stared at it in an ominous silence.

As they asked around they were told that two young people had passed in the

---

[24] Handmade patchwork blanket

direction of Kara Kol, the city on the South side of Issyk-Kul lake, gone to Chuy, headed for Kochkor in the North of Kyrgyzstan, were staying at Issyk Kul, were on their way to Kishinei village and Oi Kaiyng village, had just left for Borondoi or were on the road through the mountains to the south of Kyrgyzstan. It soon became apparent that nobody knew exactly where they had headed or where they might be. The young man had certainly shown he was a match for all the older men and as this slowly sunk in they realised further searching was futile and called off their search.

After only one year, however, carrying a little baby and the body of his dead wife the young man arrived back in the area on his horse. Ak Zyinat had given birth to a baby son, but afterwards she had been dreadfully ill and had never recovered. After burying his wife, the young man was ill for a long time. His father sought to cure him with herbs for as long as ten years, and he almost became a normal human being. He never shaved his beard and his moustache. Poor man, he passed away last year. I even forgot his name. Peace to his soul. I heard he was playing the komuz when he died. He only ever said one word "Ak Zyinat!" When the komuz fell from his hands, "Ak Zyinat, Ak Zyinat, Ak Zyinat!"sounded three times and then the strings broke…

Father crouched down on his feet, and started praying for the young man, Shaimendi, and the beauty of the girl, Sary Kyz. He dedicated his prayer to the greatest emotion of humanity: love.

"But father I still do not understand, why is Janysh the "Bad piss"? It is such a bad term to use!"

"Oh, my son! When he took Ak Zyinat away, they were not blessed. It was an unlawful union."

After a long pause he continued. "It is now early morning and I need to catch a little sleep. We all need a little time for a rest" He pulled his coat over himself and promptly fell asleep.

My father hadn't finished his story. After that year, we had supposedly moved away because it was time for me to attend school and my father had reached the age to retire. I had heard the conclusion to his life story many times: typically he would let you get comfortable then recount why he had eventually given up all horse business.

In reality, his life changed in the spring when the vet arrived from the Agricultural Science Research Institute. They had learned that my father always got through every winter without any losses in his herd of horses, and they now wanted to check the blood of the stallion, as they surmised it must be a fine pedigree. They had muttered about getting samples and setting up breeding programmes. They took away the blue-white stallion and the big mare. My Father fought with them and pleaded for them to at least let him keep them until autumn. He even started to try to take legal action.

On being asked why my father had got through winter without any losses to his herd the people who used to work with him said, "He is simply a mad religious man and his praying saves his herd". Occasionally some had laughed at him but as time went on, most of his colleagues had believed him rather than laugh at him. For the authorities, however, this wasn't an answer or a decent explanation and they did not give him his two precious horse's back, as they continued to look for a scientific answer.

When my dad was convinced he wouldn't get anywhere, he took one of the horses from his herd for himself by putting a private stamp on it, and then gave the whole herd back to the Government. The one he took was Karager. Father then moved to Jumgal. All the while he took very good care of this animal: he rested him during the winter and rode him only for a short while in the warm summer weather.

Later, when I joined the Army, the government people returned. It transpired that they couldn't find scientific reasons for the good health of his herd, and his herd was not now performing any better than any of the other herds. This was annoying them and they were convinced he was holding back information from the Union. In an act of jealous retribution they enacted an order that they required his mare, and took away Karager. As my father fought to get his beloved horse back from them he learned that the authorities had sent it to the meat factory, where it had been slaughtered.

When I returned from the Army, my mother cried and told me that my father had given up trying to be a hero and had resigned himself to leading a simple life and aging.

Karager! What a fine, fine animal: he used to run for several days and nights and never tired!

The Kyrgyz have a saying: "The horse is wings!" This is a fitting epitaph for a horse like our Karager!

CHAPTER 4

STORY OF ALIEN

How the Alien defends his actions.
  - Who are you?
  - The light of hope is green,
  - Life's colour changes by seasons.
  - The story has to be told to the future generation as a reminder of
the stories of times past.

When I woke up next morning the sun was just coming up.

It was the first time I had slept well for years. I decided I was not going to go jogging today: instead I would do something meaningful. Mother and father were returning after having tied up two young foals near the river. They were arguing about something and I could hear father protesting a point. I listened, and understood that he was winning mother over to preparing a gift for our Beggar.

In the little pasture the Beggar was shaking his Asa Musa stick and trying to round up some sheep.

I got up quickly, and went over to the little river: it was clean, fresh and cool, and it reflected as clearly as a mirror. I washed my face then returned to the house, where I stirred the kymys in its little black pot before pouring it into a glass to take outside to drink.

My parents were patiently waiting for the Beggar near the house, but he was still trying to prove his worth as a shepherd.

"Father, I will run the sheep away up to the mountains. I will use your horse and tie mine up in the shade for a little while, because when I get back I'll be going to the Karala-Aska. Please say goodbye to your Holy Man for me."

"Hmm, what business do you have there?"

"I will resolve it today with the Farm Head. I will get him to say 'Yes' or 'No'".

"Take care, my son. Remember 'anger is the devil, intelligence is the friend'. Please think it all over very carefully. Your left hand's anger can be steadied by a calm right hand - you should know that. Don't go: it wouldn't be worth it in the frame of mind you are in. Maybe I will go instead: it is my right to help my son! When the Farm Head sees me and we talk, he might change his mind about sending you to study, or he may find a young shepherd instead,"

"No, I will go myself" I was strong and confident. "After our sheep have lambed there are always some losses. I should report it myself, discuss the whys and hows, and how I have calculated things. I will explain it all and have everything confirmed. If you go, the farm accountant will mess around with you and nothing will be agreed," I said with a calm voice.

"I see. In that case you can go. Do not act like you do at home, behave yourself, and don't get hurt. Don't fight anyone," said my father, though I could see he was worried about me going to see the Farm Head.

I replied "Don't worry; I will be as diplomatic as I can."

The Beggar arrived while we were talking and looked at us both intently before asking if everything was fine.

"Dear Holy Man, I need to take our sheep to Karala Aska as early as I can, before it gets hot and while the grass is still moist. They need the fresh grass. I cannot travel with you and I hope that you will not be angry. So now I say goodbye." And at that I stepped forward to offer my hand.

While we were shaking hands, I felt an electrical shock that coursed through my whole body. It reminded me of the shocks we used to get off the magnet in our school physics class, or from the feed wire to the engine spark plugs on the threshing machine we used to muck about with as kids. We used to fight when we were small to get a chance to touch the wire and feel the charge, as we were told that that sort of power would not do us any harm. I was smiling and remembering my childhood when I got the electric shock from the Beggar's hand... When my father saw this he said in a rush:

"Holy Man, please come inside,"

I told my father: "Please, I will be back before noon." I was sure I would have enough time to talk with Silem. After that I would have time to go on to the village and bring the sheep down as well.

After I had herded our sheep down from the mountain, ready to move them on to the Karala Aska, I set off up into the high mountains. As I scrambled up the final section to the place where the Soul of the Mountains grows I came across Silem. He was waiting for me quietly and calmly on the same stone he had sat on yesterday. I, on the other hand, was breathing heavily and sweating as if I had drunk a lot of tea.

"Ah, my Holy Man. How did you arrive here so quickly and how long have you been waiting?"

Silem smiled at me and showed me his magic stick, his Asa Musa.

"Well then, start talking now," I said, as I wiped the sweat from my forehead. I sat down with my legs folded up tight. "I am all ears!"

"What do you want me to tell you first?"

"I would have thought that would be obvious. When you first came to Planet Earth, how you travel and why you are messing about with the people on this planet of ours. Yes, that's where you should start. Pardon me for being so blunt, my dear 'Holy Man'", I said.

"No it is fine," the Beggar smiled "there are lots of things you do not understand and I will try and explain succinctly."

He made himself comfortable by sitting down, crossing his legs, and sticking his Asa Musa in the ground beside him. Then he leaned forward, resting both elbows on his knees. As he settled he gave me the long deep stare of a being, who knows-all, and started:

"Our ancestors somehow managed to turn the corners of our Galaxy and that resulted in opening up space travel and the possibility to go to other worlds through upper space from our anti world. We found we could reach the central world, and as such we started to research all the planets of your star. When we came to this planet it was the time you know as the middle Ages, when the Spanish Inquisition was in power. At that time, some scientists had begun to emerge and were trying to find out what the Earth really looked like. However the scientists were being cruelly persecuted. Our people quickly learned to hide their scientific backgrounds, and turned themselves into Travellers, Beggars and Dervishes. That was how they spent their time on this planet as they researched it and learnt about its resources.

"Ordinary people did, however, look after our travellers well. They recognised that they were using their high educational attainment and skills to help them. They often declared that they were acting on behalf of the Almighty, and nobody guessed that they were continually using their skills to develop science. People trusted them if they felt they were acting on behalf of God! Real fanatical missionaries often turned to the Dervishes to encourage religion among ordinary people as they travelled around Planet Earth. There were a lot of others like me, trying to conduct scientific research, but they were always rumours about punishments.

"There were many cases when explorers from our planet were unable to fulfil their missions and were prevented from going home. Some of them used their Asa Musas inappropriately." Silem indicated his stick. "This is not a just a gravity generator, we also use it occasionally to materialise our bio-energy to make sure everything is all right." He held up his boneless fingers. "This boneless big finger contains useful, transformative bio-energy. Some of our spies used this power, and sometimes they were framed as demons, and badly punished by the Inquisition. Others suffered just because their flying saucers broke down. Some of them just stayed on Earth because they preferred it to sleeping in suspended animation. Others used too many active materials and could not reach their trans-rockets on time.

"The timetable for space flights was changed and they gave their permission. If they could not reach the trans-rockets in time, the law was that one would have to spend spare time in the suspended animation zone: you should already know that, I have told you many times before. And these anti-world spies who couldn't get home on time preferred to stay on Planet Earth, thereby doubling and tripling the numbers of dervishes, and beggars. Nobody could recognise them in their new positions. Some were developing astronomy to study the stars, always to know what's happening in space. Their examples were always very useful for Earth.

"There were lots of examples of Beggars surviving on Earth. Indeed it was often the case that new arrivals from our world decided to stay, and it became a "cult" that ideas and knowledge imparted by a beggar would be passed on to others. Praying, giving to charity and mutual respect are all traits that we have in our anti-world and that we have promoted here.

"You may think that we are born with a talent to talk in poetry. In actual fact we hate using our voices for conversation. Once we used to talk like human beings and had vocal conversations. Now, however, our bio-energy is so well developed that we use our brains to communicate in most circumstances, as it is so easy.

"But now on Earth, the beggar's "cult" was widespread and everybody used poetry to talk to each other.

However let us concentrate on the main topic that you want to know about."In those days the main objective was to learn from every perspective about life and nature on any other planets which were habitable. Our agents were amazed by the Solar System of the Sun. It had so many truly amazing features but the main interest was of course Planet Earth: it was found to be very well developed at that moment and time.

"We found your eastern civilizations were the best developed, and all our scientific work was done in this area, especially in Central Asia, where we discovered a lot of scientific material that we wanted to understand.

"However one important thing occurred in one of the early expeditions. The captain fell very ill, with some unknown illness for which we had no cure. That was the main reason why the expedition decided to stay on Earth. They were worried not only about the captain but also about the possibility that the unknown illness might spread to others. The disease was unlike anything we had encountered on our own planet, and we did not know any cures or treatments for it.

Illnesses that we couldn't cure, broken bones that wouldn't heal and coughing that wouldn't stop often developed from this unknown illness. This was often the case for those who flew often through space, and if someone was diagnosed with this illness they were prohibited from flying back to our homeland.

So when the leader of this expedition fell ill with this unknown illness, they touched their ship down in Ming Bulak[25]. At that same time a man who had been exploring that area, and seemed to know Ming Bulak quite well, arrived. He was drinking water from a little spring when something accidentally dropped from his pocket into the water. It turned out to be a small purse, and he pulled it out of the water and set about transferring the contents to a dry purse. As he was doing this he became involved in our story, as he was holding two pieces of meat that were slowly dissolving in his hands.

As he moved a little way back up the stream he pulled out another two small pieces of meat and dipped them into the spring. Then he stared at them. Nothing happened. He was mystified and so he moved to the exact spot where he had been before and tried again. This time the meat dissolved like before. He looked long and hard at the spot and then he saw it: a small white flower was growing from the stream's bank. He picked the flower and touched his dried meat with it, and the meat completely melted away. For a moment he stood still, not quite understanding what he was seeing and not understanding what this flower was or where it had come from. Mystified, he started walking along beside the spring water.

---

[25] A lake in the Kyrgyz Tian Shian Mountains. Translates as a Thousands of water springs ie an area which collects spring water from all over Tian- Shian' mountains

He came across a large stone where two small children, a boy and a girl, were playing at being husband and wife. They had laid a tablecloth over the stone, and had covered it with herbs. The girl had a little crown on her head, made of the little white flowers which the man had found by the spring earlier, and the boy had a belt of the herbs which grew all around. When they saw the man watching them with a look of amazement on his face and seeming utterly lost they stopped playing and stared at him.

"Daughter, that crown you have made: what is the name of the flower?" asked the man. The girl looked at the boy and they walked closer to him and replied "It is Soul of the Mountains. We picked them from around that big stone and we made this crown ourselves."

"We are playing husband and wife. That's why my dear Nyraim made me a belt from a different herb, the one we call Kekire. Can you see how she made it? There are six different strands, all of different lengths and twisted together to make a belt with a very strong hook."

The man was relieved that the children weren't afraid and were talking to him. He continued: "Can I see how well you have made your crown and belt. I will grade you on how well you have done!" The boy and girl looked at each other suspiciously. But the children were typical Kyrgyz youngsters and had grown up with deep respect for their elders. They quickly and freely took off their herb creations and handed them over to the man. He was suitably impressed with their beautiful handiwork. As he held them he took some more of the dried meat from his pocket and put a little piece on each of the two objects. As he watched, both pieces of the meat melted away. He passed the belt and the crown back to the children and thanked them profusely. Then he looked to the heavens and slowly the tears rolled from his eyes as he pulled on his white beard.

The little boy asked, "Why are you crying?"

The man looked down and even though he was crying, he smiled: "I think these herbs are marvellous. They may be able to cure the illness that has taken people like my daughter-in-law and my son. Kekire and Edelweiss are fantastic! Both herbs are wonderful!"

Just then two beggars arrived. Their arrival made the old man calm down and he stopped crying. He then told them a story:

"My name is Ulukman; I try to serve as a herbal doctor in this area. My son grew up very spoiled and wild. The day after his marriage, he told his wife 'My father can bring dead people back to life. If you trust me, we will drink this melted goat fat which will kill us, and then my father will bring us back to life.' And so they both drank too much melted goat fat: it was lying in our house as I was planning to use it to prepare medicines.

"I was working in one of our outhouses when I suddenly heard my wife screaming "Vai-dat. God help us!' I knew something terrible had happened as I entered the house. I found her standing in a trance in my herb room next to the dead bodies of my son and daughter-in-law. I tried to bring them back from the dead with every skill I had and with every herb and potion I had ever come across, but they had injured themselves beyond anything I could heal, and I could not do anything. Their hearts and lungs were full of solidified goat fat which wouldn't melt with anything I tried.

I kept two little pieces of goat fat-affected flesh from their hearts. Since then I have picked millions of herbs and plants to try to find something to melt the flesh. I have tried for such a long time and now suddenly I find that both Edelweiss and Kekire can dissolve these two pieces of flesh.

Only these two herbs melt away the goat fat. Why I didn't think to try these before? I should give up being an herbal doctor! Edelweiss is known to cure thousands of illnesses. I should have thought of that and seen if it would dissolve goat fat as well."

After his sad story, the two beggars took him from the top of the mountain to their space ship, where the captain was ill. Ulukman checked his pulse and declared, "Seven herbs for thousands of illness, three are the same, and there is only one key."

This severely aroused Melis' curiosity, and he interrupted Silem "What is that: this 1000-7(3)-1? I have heard these numbers before!"

Silem patiently explained: "The seven is for the seven herbs that are good for a thousand illness, these are Ak Kodol, Eremen, Shybak, Shyraljyn, Uu-korgoshun, Koko Meren and Edelweiss. The three means that the first three – Eremen, Shybak and Shyraljyn - can be substituted for each other: if one is not available another can be used. The one key means that without Edelweiss the herbs are useless."

"I understand now. What happened then?" asked Melis.

"Then Ulukman, the herbal doctor, went to see the captain with his unknown illness. He got some of the beggars to fetch him water from Ming Bulak, boiled the seven herbs and gave the infusion to the captain. In some time he was cured, much to the amazement of both Ulukman and the beggars.

"That place Ming Bulak is now known as Suusamyr! That means it is a precious place where not many illnesses are found. Edelweiss really is the "soul of the mountains", and the water seems to have magical properties as well. After that, Ming Bulak became known as Suusamyr or 'Holy Water'. And everyone else who flies here from neighbouring stars called this place Suusamyr as well!

"The crew and scientists from that expedition took the cure for the 'incurable illness' back to our homeland to help cure others, and our people were very thankful.

"There has been excellent scientific research conducted on our planet into these seven herbs and other similar herbs which grow there, but Uu Korgoshyn was never found. We soon recognised that because we do not have any eclipses on our planet, even plants close in composition are still no use at all.

How often we wanted to take the roots of Edelweiss and Uu Korgoshyn. We tried to use all our skills, and conducted many experiments with our highly developed power! But we only recently started harvesting of Uu Korgoshyn on our planet! Edelweiss didn't grow on our anti-world at all.

"Before that we gathered Uu Korgoshun very often on planet Earth.

"Last night your father told me about the blue-white stallion, I knew that horse so well.

"I used to work in this area, collecting Uu Korgoshun. In those days there wasn't any medicine which could relieve Tutok[26], and we only discovered it recently. We used to gather Uu Korgoshun in early winter, and used to get Tutok when we arrived on Earth. We needed to find a solution quickly to help ourselves. Not long ago, Kyrgyz men travelling along high mountain roads had Tutok and nosebleeds, and fell unconscious, but then often recovered, stood up and continued on their way. We often saw this. It seems that your pedigree horses' perspiration works like oxygen. When I discovered this, they added me to the search party for Soul of the Mountains.

"Last night your dad spoke of how he went to the Kazakh village and someone gave him a signal and called on the doctor Turusbek for help. I don't know exactly who it was, but I presume it was one of ours picking Ermen, Ak Kodol or Kokomeren. The blue-white stallion arrived because at the time when the mare was poisoned, our new agents, who had come to

---

[26] An illness related to high blood pressure

pick Uu Korgoshun, were suffering from Tutok. I separated him from the others. But when I saw how the horse-people were struggling I had to pass on the blue-white stallion without raising suspicion. Even my own friend was suffering but, because I helped avert a disaster for the local people, I was given the right to visit Earth any time I wanted. That night, when the blue-white mare chewed the wolf's head off, I took the blue-white stallion away. When you pick Uu Korgoshun, Tutok strikes you a lot, we used to be exhausted. But only pure pedigree horses' perspiration is useful for breathing, and we used it many times.

"I see. When Seyit fell from his horse, it was you who gave the signal to my father?"

"Yes, I often met your father."

"All right. All right. You two met each many times, I am not arguing with that. It would be better if you told me why the horses have a light in their ears?"

Well, pure pedigree horses light up on dark nights, that is true, but not every one of them emits that light. It may be the result of electrical energy which develops like when women who are very proud of themselves dress up in pure white silk. It may be that it is something to do with phosphorus inside their ears or some level of their brains. We have not been able to discover this secret either yet, but maybe we will in the future…"

"Of course, the future is great, is there still a lot to discover?"

"Yes, that's right, Melis, there are plenty of secrets to be uncovered in the future. The past, as well, is full of secrets."

"And what are you planning to do now?"

"We will never try to rob you, nor would it even cross our minds. This is a very desperate act. We will sort it out. Maybe when the time comes we will help you in return. Look, take you for example. As your father told us, because of our involvement you were cured of Kara San – you sometimes call this cancer."

"When I was ill?" I asked

"Turusbek the herbal doctor wasn't worried about you for nothing. When you were lying for two days in the field, he knew it would be something very serious, and that's why he cured you, before that terrible illness took its course. He may be a grandson of the Ulukman who helped cured our ancestors."

"'Uncured illness', 'Karasan', 'Cancer': what is this difference between these three?"

"It is all the same, actually. It manifests itself in different ways, but essentially it is all the same."

I badly wanted to quiz Silem about all sorts of things, but I held myself back thinking that I would ask him a lot more next time, when we were not in such a rush. The day was moving on – it was already afternoon. My dad would arrive soon in the pasture below with the sheep and my horse. This meant I could challenge Silem on only one important subject. Yes, only one crucial issue!"

"Well, Silem, the 'uncured illness' is now very widespread on Earth. Medical science has developed quickly but this 'uncured illness' remains resilient and there is nothing we can do about it. The herbal medicine you used and showed us in the time of the Inquisition, and the treatment that Ulukman performed, is no longer used: it has been utterly forgotten. Nowadays the 'key' is as important for us human beings as oxygen and water. In order to have the right to pick Edelweiss reinstated, you need to bring the key to cure the 'incurable illness' and the formula for the '1000-7-(3)-1'.

Silem stood silent listening intently.

"You will decide for yourselves but you have learned from this planet how to cure this 'incurable illness and now it is time for repayment for this. We may have known in the past but now we have forgotten and you should teach us again. I beg you, on behalf of my planet and humanity, I beg you!" said Melis.

My beggar stood up and looked at me with great sincerity. Almost as if he was talking to himself he whispered:

"These are precious requests. I shall tell this to our nineteen white beards, which make the decisions. I cannot answer you now, but I will try to fulfil your 'precious request' and use our ethical law to argue for this and to succeed."

I stood up as well. "Will we see each other again two years from now?"

"Inshallah, God Willing," he replied.

Silem took his Asa Musa, raised it high, and used it to call his flying saucer. As the craft approached he wrapped his flying raincoat tight and moved off towards it. I didn't wait till he was flying away: I went down to round up my sheep.

CHAPTER 5
THE AUTHOR'S STORY

Soul of the Mountain, will you grow in cold weather?
Will you come back to me?
Like a rain shower?
It cannot be reached
If I did discover how to find it
I would leave it.
My story to the village of love…

The weather was starting to change. Clouds were forming around the mountains and the wind was getting up. Those who had been drinking champagne were starting to feel the cold. The group of friends, who had been listening carefully to Melis' story, now seemed to be losing interest, so he concentrated on finishing the story quickly.

"It looks like you have had enough of my story. I could tell you how the Head of the Collective Farm and I never agreed on a solution. I tried my best to argue, and the arguments went outside the office, showing the real story of the falsifications that the Farm Head had made. Even though these were proved and he was prosecuted, I was also punished, disqualified from being a shepherd for one year because I allegedly didn't report at the appointed time how many sheep had lived and how many died after the winter and spring. I don't want to tell you all the little details of this part of my life, and how I fought back. It is much better if I tell you about the anti-world people and my precious request.

"Two years later Silem did come back: it is all to do with the distance from Earth around the various levels to his anti-world and the movement of stars. That meant that the quickest he could travel there and back was two years: one year in each direction.

"Silem had told me that a trans-rocket flies ten times faster than the speed of light and that when they are in hyperspace, these spaceships fly a hundred times faster! Even at that speed it still takes two years to reach its destination and return.

"And now, after Silem came back to Earth we met and he told me

"Our Nineteen white beards held a meeting about passing on the knowledge surrounding that one herb and the medicine it can make. Our planet which still fears war and conflict does not give permission to take anything by force – being one of our basic Ethical Laws. The decision they came to was that if they were not granted permission to pick more Edelweiss the answer would be 'no'; if they were granted permission then the answer would be 'yes'.

"This suggestion was supported by our Government, Education and Culture, Agriculture Ministries. Environmental scientists stated that without Soul of the Mountains, there would sooner or later be a lot of dead with the 'incurable disease'. This would lead to the medicinal remedy, the '1000-7(3)-1' preparation being forgotten about forever. The Nineteen white beards certainly couldn't allow this to happen for either world and as such deemed that it was a very sensible decision. After a long discussion, it was decided that the secrets would be given to just one person on planet Earth. That person should be sufficiently educated and be ready to cure the 'incurable disease' and make his own medicine, to be useful for humanity and the whole planet.

"Silem had suggested my candidature to be this one person on Earth. He had explained that to transfer the knowledge they would have to do this by a biological method using a potion made from Edelweiss. If I wanted to progress with this I would have to agree to Silem returning to his homeland with four more Edelweiss plants that were ripe and ready to go. What should I say to him?

"I thought about it and agreed of course. And he is going to come back next year. Before I know the outcome, I can't give the Soul of the Mountains to Rena, and that's why I couldn't get married," said Melis. Then he looked around at everybody.

There was an unpleasant silence.

"When did you start writing such wonderful science fiction?" asked Alybai, as he looked at Melis with mistrust. He continued in his sarcastic tone: "Will you give it to newspapers and magazines first, or go straight to Berdi to have it published as a book instead?"

"Really, that's a very good idea. If you brush it up a bit, it will be a pretty good story!" Tyko added

"Is it made up or true?" Berdi asked, as he took his glasses off to clean them. "Which is it?"

"You made our day very interesting with this bullshit you are telling us. What else do you want to say?" asked Rena, as she started collecting her stuff to go home.

"Dear friends. It is a true story: I didn't add a thing. Please believe me. Next year we could have a cure which will help the whole of humanity. Nature hasn't been able to produce it, but we will have it very soon! And then..."

"Then what?" demanded Alybai.

"Then me and Rena...'"

"Horse shit!" Alybai stood up with his teeth clenched. "Are you going to marry Rena? No!"

"I said I need one more year," said Melis, almost pleading

In an instant Alybai let fly with a clenched fist that smashed into Melis's face.

Melis did not want a fight but now he was flat on his back and totally vulnerable to the others massing around him, so he just lay there for a while, at their mercy. As he tried to stand up, Tyko punched him on the neck and pushed his' face into the grass in front of Rena. The drivers, standing nearby, rushed in to stop the fight.

Rena was trying to say something, but she couldn't. She started crying out, staring at him. Then, she stood up, went to her car and sat inside. The driver, who had been holding Tyko left him, went straight to his car and drove away immediately.

"Fool!" screamed Alybai as he freed himself from his brother-in-law's arms and went straight to his car.

Tyko stood up, shook the dust from his jacket and looked towards Berdi. "Let's go to the car. It is time to go. This man will meet his new friends from a non-existent planet and go home in a non-existent flying saucer.

Berdi wasn't so sure. "Go and wait for me near the deep pool where we swim. I will have a word with him," he said.

Melis and Berdi walked side by side. In five minutes they reached the pool and during that period Berdi asked just one question:

"Was it all true?"

Melis said simply "Yes".

As they reached the pool Berdi said "Let's go. I shall give you a lift?"

Melis looked at Berdi with begging eyes. "No, thank you. I need some fresh air. I am losing my senses. I need to walk. Rain will refresh me."

At that Melis clapped Berdi on the back and walked off, fast and alone.

Behind him he heard Tyko swearing at him. Melis was angry. He remembered the time he had beaten them all up and he felt he wanted to do the same again. Then the rain started. Melis could not tell whether it was his tears or rain that was running warm across his face. He couldn't tell the difference, he didn't care, and he certainly didn't care about the three cars quietly heading away behind him...

Sometime later, Melis was lying on his stomach staring at the letter. Suddenly something dripped onto it. He looked up at a clear blue sky but he knew it was a tear from his eye.

"Damn, this is the third time. Just when I thought my feelings had gone," thought Melis. "Now I can't be so sure." In that instant he decided to leave his sheep at home that evening and travel to Frunze...

This was his last decision as a chief shepherd after two days of struggling with his ideas.

After the events of the previous year, Melis hadn't kept in touch with any of his friends, and he had not heard anything about them. The letter from Berdi outlined how Rena had been in Pobeda village in autumn to pass a red flag medal to the Farm Head. There had been an electrical accident in the farm garage. As she helped them deal with the fire there was a petrol tank explosion and she was severely burned. She had been in the district hospital for almost two months, and then returned to Frunze.

Nobody had realised that after six months a tumour had developed in her burnt skin. Now she was in the Cancer Research Department at the Main Hospital in Frunze.

Melis had been told a short version of the story by Berdi while he was driving him to the city.

"When I wrote to you it was not too serious. Now it is not good. It looks like she only has a few days left to live. The doctors have all but given up and are searching for her relatives to take her home," said Berdi sadly. "Did you know Rena is an orphan? She hasn't got anyone, just us – her friends. I was talking to my wife and we would like to take care of her, but Rena is stubborn."

"It looks like my words meant something to her, or else she was upset. I don't know, she cried a lot."

"'Can I make one or two requests?' she said.

"I was sitting beside her and listening carefully. I turned the light up a little bit and we spoke.

"'When you bury me, please just give me a smooth little stone with six verses of poetry inscribed.'

"At Rena's request, I lifted her pillow and saw a white paper napkin. It was very hard to look. With a heavy heart, I picked it up carefully.

"'You will find it easy to do these things, for friendship's sake. I know you will do them. Copy what is written in this poem word for word onto the stone. Don't write my name on the stone as then they would then just be like any other words in the graveyards. That is my first request.'

"'Secondly: I spent too long with Komsomol and I ignored my poems and writings. I completely forgot about them, but I have written books of poems. Please publish them. People should know my name. All my paperwork is in my flat. You will find it. Are you going to do what I ask?'

-"Of course I will"-Berdi had told her. "May be, I don't think, I had been so sure of anything "- continued Berdi.

Rena still speaking with calm voice: " So, now my third request........"

"I don't think I had ever been so sure of anything so now my third request. Yesterday I asked my colleagues that they take my body to Sokuluk[27]. Please don't ever show Melis where I am buried.' She finished by saying to me 'Leave now and never come to see me again. Stay in touch only from outside. Goodbye. If I did anything wrong in my life, please forgive me.'

Berdi stopped speaking.

In my mind, Rena was looking at me and smiling "Please, could you read me your 'Love and the Traveller' poem. I don't remember its details. She was almost begging me.

I recited this poem to Rena from memory, as much as I could remember.

Shadow of the mountains…
Night…
Culture is riding a horse,
Rushing on ahead to be in love…
The homeland where the high gorges are
The bird is crying, and stops.

There are vast rivers
Cascading their sound through the mountains

---

[27] *A small town outside Bishkek*

To Kapchigai, from Kapchigai
Never ending.
There is a fire,
You see it far away
The traveller is surrounded
The fire is burning but there is no steel to melt...

My destiny is to be a traveller,
Looking for love in this life.
Maybe we shall meet somewhere.
Very much like you, and beautiful.

My heart is like an empty space
I loved a girl, no doubt.
But she is not there any more
No point to hide it...

But it is life's miracle
Your feelings get stronger.
Couldn't find a beauty with smoky eyes
To rip out my heart and take it away

She was listening very carefully - like the first time. As I finished she said only one thing. "So only now you understand what love meant."

Berdi started talking again: "After that she didn't let anybody go to see her. I sent the letter to you. I hope she will be a little happier before she passes away."

Melis wiped his sweat away from his eyebrows. "Do you have that poem with you, the one she gave to you to put on her grave?" he asked.

Berdi pulled a piece of paper from his pocket. "I typed it up," he said and handed Melis the poem.

Melis was shaking, and couldn't open it for a while. Then he did. He didn't see the words: instead in his mind's eye he saw Rena singing a song, beautiful and kind.

I have waited for you all my life
I thought you would come to me,
I have given up now,
My hope is gone.
I have gone and I will never return to you
I will always be thinking of you,
Sadly now I am ill
I never could openly express myself
I am dying now of love.

There used to be fire in me
But this feeling will be gone soon
I will never see you in my dreams
I will sleep forever.

I will never see you in my dreams...
Flowers will bloom on my grave.
Even then I will be faithful to you...
The cloud in the sky
Will cry from time to time.

Be brave and sing a song
Life is beautiful, enjoy it!
I am gone. I leave for you
The pleasure of life....
You know who I am:
I am not going to write my name.

In his mind Melis saw himself standing facing a bright red field, almost a desert of red. And in that red flourish there was only one grave. There in the sunset someone in red was riding a horse.

Both Melis and Berdi went into the hospital and up to the second floor.

"Oh no, not that woman! She asked not to be disturbed. She was very angry" said the duty nurse, who was obviously uncomfortable with the situation. "If you still want to see her, please go with the Deputy Director of the hospital. She will only listen to him, no one else."

114

Melis and Berdi went downstairs to find the Deputy Director. He was in his early forties: a little blond haired chubby man hurrying around a ward. They got him to sit down and listen to them very carefully, he didn't say 'yes' or 'no' but stood up and gestured for them to follow him. Rena apparently was alone in her room: when they reached the door he spoke:

"Only this woman's boyfriend should go inside," and he indicated at Melis with his chin. "She has asked that we should not let anybody into her room, isn't that right brother Berdi? I know all of you now except this young man, and that is why he should go in. Maybe Rena is expecting him."

Melis went into the room and nearly screamed. Two strange eyes were waiting for him, someone unknown, looking like a hungry ghost. She started moving her lips and jaw, and slowly the words came out. "Finally, you are here!"

Melis was struggling to say something, and finding it difficult even to breathe, as if a bone was stuck in his throat. He shook his head.

"You should forgive me, Melis." The voice sounded like it was coming from underground, eerie to hear.

"Life is short; we care about stupid things and waste a lot of time. That last time I shouldn't have been so upset about the Edelweiss, I should have put a white scarf on my own head and stayed at your house, marrying myself to you..."[28]

"... When you entered this room, you were scared weren't you? Once I was so beautiful. Am I now? Now, you cannot live like that, you should get married, please! Nowadays all the girls are beautiful, aren't they? Choose someone and get married. This is my only request for you: I beg you.

"I was crazy about you, I was drawn to you like a butterfly but I couldn't make either of us happy, able to take pleasure from life. Now I am passing away.

"Don't repeat my mistake. My foolishness is enough for both of us. Stop looking for ideals. You should be human, have a house, love and be loved. Have

---

[28] In Kyrgyz tradition, when a new daughter- in-law arrives for the first time the oldest woman in the house covers her head with a white scarf, as a symbol of her lawful acceptance

kids - lots of children and lots of grandchildren. Don't waste your life. Will you promise me this: will you? Promise me three times!"

"I will… I will… I will…" said Melis.

"Oh, thank God, I feel much better. That makes me feel free. I am very grateful to you – you gave me your benediction."

Melis went out of room. In the hallway Berdi was speaking to the doctor. "Please, tell me doctor, how many days does she still have to live?

"Why do you need to know?"

"I need to know" replied Melis harshly

The doctor sighed and replied "Perhaps between a week and ten days."

"I have time then." said Melis.

"Doctor, please, I am begging you; try to keep her alive at least one more week. In one week, this girl and I are getting married!"

The Deputy Director looked at him with deep sympathy, "Poor man, he seems utterly crazy: psychological problems" He was very quiet and walked away shaking his head and pulling a strange face.

When they got outside Berdi asked him in a very calm voice "What are you going to do in one week? Or is the man from that anti-world going to visit you?"

"Yes!!! I reckon it is time now; they should be here any day. This is the time when the Soul of the Mountains is blooming! How can I get back: will there be any seats on the night bus?"

Berdi was astonished. He looked at Melis as if he saw him for the first time in his life. He shook his head in disgust and spat with anger. With hatred in his heart he turned and walked away.

Melis understood that Berdi had been the last of his trusted friends. Now he had lost him too.

CHAPTER 6

THE GORGE WHERE THE EDELWEISS FLOURISHES

Space is limitless
What is the point of that?
If you don't make any changes in your life
Even God cannot help you
Therefore you should change your own destiny…

Clever or foolish
You cannot control happiness
What is that?
You don't worry about that!

As the alien spaceship approached Earth, Silem was summoned to the bridge.

One of the nineteen Elders started speaking. "Silem, we have made our decision, it is done. After our arrival we will have to quickly depart on the same day or else our super-space trans-rocket won't be able to reach the transit point on time.

"Our teachings about the incurable illnesses will be transferred by the pharmacological method: that is the only way that will allow him to get to work very quickly. You know that the teaching of our ways on such topics is generally against our ethical law and principles. However we are going break these. We have been given permission to do this for the people of Earth. This is a major decision, and very important, and it is why I am here myself.

"The pharmacological method is through a bio-electric transfer. It is a three stage process and should be completed in three days. We agree to give this information to Melis. However it will only be Melis who receives it as he and he alone has the right to know.

"Now, we were waiting for him for three days and now, we don't want to waste our time anymore. So, you should go and see him and start the process...."

"This is the last chance for mankind to survive and reach the results for themselves. You stay here and wait for Melis. When he arrives, let him drink the contents of this small blue vial," said the elder, who was wearing a large conical hat, a beautiful and amazing overcoat and long thigh-length boots, and carrying an ornate Asa Musa stick.

"Tell him that his existing memory will vanish and his physical body is going to be transformed to that of a sixteen year old. He will only remember his life up to when he was sixteen years old. The neuro-programme method will insert a synthesis programme in his brain to allow him to make medicines for the incurable illness.

"These future achievements will make the treatment a success. After he has graduated from high school, he will go to medical school and then he will discover secrets of medicine that will help him cure the uncured illness. After that he will encourage further scientific research or undertake it himself. If he refuses to do this, to make these future achievements, and does not want such success then the last option will be used: you will drink the liquid yourself and dedicate your life to saving humanity."

Silem was shaking as he was passed the little blue vial.

"This vial will also work on your body. It will make you like a sixteen year-old boy again. Please, take this very seriously Silem. We are educated and we really believe in such things! Ethical law systems are like that, my dear Silem!

"Who knows, maybe after you return to that age you could become an herbal doctor like Ulukman."

The beggar with the ornate Asa Musa stick took three shining stars from his chest pocket and gave them to Silem.

If you are going to stay on Earth, your anti-world mind and power will slowly vanish, but these talisman will help you in times of great hardship. It will support you, and prevent you from getting depressed. It has extra bio-energy for you that will help you out.

But, if everything goes well and you return to our home in the near future, you will take my place. Our ethical laws will have been adhered to and your punishment will have finished by doing this. Not only will that but by following our ethics and demonstrating how these can be adhered to you have the right to become one of the Nineteen Aksakals of our planet, replacing me.

Try to get back to the trans-rocket orbit. From there you could have a chance to reach the homeland later. In the meanwhile you should wait for the next spaceship in suspended animation.

I will tell the nineteen elders that you should stay as an Agent, and they will not fire you.

They called a flying saucer transfer ship, and at that the Elder disappeared. As Silem arrived on Earth, he took up his persona of a beggar, but in fact he was now a real beggar! He started walking towards Melis's home.

That same day Melis reached home before sunset. As he entered his yurt he saw Silem sitting and drinking kymys: he was very happy to see him.

"Did you bring it?" he asked the Beggar straightaway, not even remembering to say hello. His old father and mother were shocked that their son seemed to have completely forgotten his manners.

Silem spoke silently to Melis using his telepathic skills to let him know what his Elders had decided, and that time was of the essence as it was going to take three days to give Melis the powers – the powers he needed to save Rena.

"Let's go then, beggar," said Melis.

He was in such a rush that he left his whip hanging on the wall – something a right-thinking Kyrgyz shepherd would never do!

"Father, I have to return immediately to the city. Please try and look after the sheep yourself. We will go together now. Please take care of the house as well."

His father was somewhat astounded, and only managed to blurt out: "But tomorrow we were going to separate the sheep from the lambs!"

"Why not ask your nephew to help? He can assist you," said Melis.

The road to Kok Jol was windy, and as the two of them talked their clothes were flapping in the wind. On the way Melis recounted the situation with Rena, and how she was now lying in the hospital with the incurable illness slowly seeping away her life. Silem recounted his meeting with the Nineteen Elders, and how he had been given permission to transfer knowledge about the incurable illness to Melis as a token of gratitude for letting them take the Edelweiss.

"Well that's it my beggar," said Melis. "Whatever you are going to do you have to do it now, to save Rena's life."

Silem replied "I realise it is important. I am very grateful for the help you have given me and that is why I am here now to repay your kindness. You must, however, understand what is going to happen as I give you the knowledge you seek."

Silem pulled the little blue vial of liquid from under his robes and continued: "This liquid has been made especially for your body. As you drink it and the transfer begins it will change your brain, both now and in the future. Not only will it allow you to go and cure this 'incurable illness', it will also help your brain develop remedies and medicines in the future. Your body and mind will be like those of a sixteen year old again, and everything that has happened to you since that age will be removed from your memory forever."

Melis stopped and said: "When Rena was sixteen years old she wasn't ill with cancer! We could give her the vial! Say 'yes', Silem!"

"But she could be ill in twelve years! This is not what I was told to do!" said Silem.

"That's as may be. But we are not going to listen to your elders any more. They have left, and so many ethical laws have been broken already. We should do what we think is best! What do you suggest then?" asked Melis.

"Drink this and you will find out the 'secret' in the future," said Silem.

"This will help girls like Rena in the future. But we think Rena has only one week of life left. What if she dies before it starts working?" demanded Melis.

"In my opinion this pharmacological method will require just three days, no longer. You are relatively young and this should be only the blink of an eye. Even if it does not allow you to save Rena, you will gain some valuable experience. If you give it to Rena then you will be giving up all the future scientific achievements you are meant to have!"

"That's right!" said Melis his mind made up.

Silem saw it was pointless arguing and replied, "Well how can we now help cure Rena?"

"Well, we will go with your flying saucer to Karala Aska, in Kapchigai, where you will wait for me. I will take a taxi and arrange Rena's discharge from hospital. Then we will then drive back in the same taxi to Kapchigai, from where we will send the car away, and we will fly back in your flying saucer."

Silem agreed.

"And we will go to the cave just under where the Edelweiss is flowering, and start to help Rena."

"Good thinking," said Silem.

"Well, call your flying saucer," said Melis.

Behind Karala Aska there was an eagle's nest and in the little cave underneath this, Melis and Silem set up their little experimental hospital.

After the girl drank the blue liquid, she lay unconscious for three days, and only opened her eyes on the fourth day. Looking around the cave with amazement, she saw a slim tall Beggar standing there along with a shaven-headed young man she had never seen before.

"Who are you?" was the first question she asked, quickly followed by: "This is my cave, how did you get in here?"

Silem and Melis stood looking at each other.

"Your cave?" both asked at the same time.

"Yes! And no-one else's! I have been coming here for three summers during the holidays. I live in this cave and I look after the sheep in the fields below. Before me, no human being ever lived in this cave."

"What do you mean?" asked Melis surprised. "I used to come here too."

"You? Who are you?"

"Melis."

"Are you sure?" demanded Rena

Melis replied "Yes of course, my name is Melis!"

"My name is Melis too!"

Melis was taken aback and tried to argue "No. That is not true!"

Rena was having none of it and stated, "Yes, it is very true."

Melis tried to make sense of it and asked: "Is your father's name Uzagaaly, and your mother's Sonun?"

Rena was getting terse. "Yes, I know who my parents are! My father and mother sent you two here to search for me, but I am not going home. Anyway, I am upset and out of favour just now as I argued with my father, and we don't talk now."

Melis' eyes were rolling in their sockets, and he ended up staring at Silem. As the silence intensified, Silem sent a telepathic message "I am very sorry, Melis. We have made a very big mistake. I've been checking all the biological factors. The blue medicine was made for your personal biological signature and is only suitable for you. Rena's hormones have picked this up and have completely changed her biology from a female to a male. To a male like you! Even I cannot stop this process!"

Even as Melis struggled to grasp what Silem was saying he continued: "We are well into the whole embryonic process; her body has changed to a male body. I now have to alter her mind or else when she recovers and finds she is no longer a girl she will be completely devastated. I am going to program your childhood into her mind. I have to erase all traces from her mind that she was once female.

"Rena will have to start a new life based on starting from the age of sixteen. Rena, or is it Melis, is now twelve years younger and male. She may not even have recovered from the 'incurable illness.' She may get ill again later, after three days or three months. If that is the case I have to be ruthless. There is only one way Rena-Melis can be totally cured. When we travel, we are given a portion of medicine just in case we contract the 'incurable illness' while we are flying and travelling between worlds. That medicine is developed once for all of us. I have never had this illness and I still have my medicine. We should give it to her"

Silem looked at Rena/Melis and quietly said, "Please sleep. I will give you some medicine to help."

The 'young boy' stood up and discovered he was wearing a girl's clothes. He looked around the cave and saw strange and unfamiliar items - a strange blue light, several scientific books on the table and a framed picture of a woman. He was even more amazed than he had been the last time he had awoken.

"Are you two all right or is there something wrong with you? Yesterday when I came here there wasn't any of this stuff here. I was here sleeping on a bed I had made for myself, of grass. How did I end up in this hospital bed? Or maybe you are the 'holy' people my grandfather used to tell me about? Please be honest and tell me the truth, I am a little confused now, to say the least."

Melis picked up the framed photograph and took it over to the baffled Rena/Melis who stared at it. Then she asked: "Who is this in this picture?"

"Don't you know her?"

"No."

"Well have a good look at yourself in the mirror," replied Melis.

"Wow! That is so strange. I look like that girl?" said Rena/Melis half affirming and half asking Melis, as she looked at him with honest curiosity. "I thought I looked like you! Why do I look like the girl in the photo?"

Silem responded calmly and compassionately "For now, please drink this medicine. Uncle Melis will explain everything later. Now you need to go back to sleep. You will know everything when the time is right."

Rena/Melis was upset but she obeyed the older man's orders and lay back and soon drifted off to sleep. It wasn't until three days later that she woke. During that time she was looked after attentively by Silem and Melis. As she woke up, they brought her new clothes and as she studied her surroundings her confusion returned. Before she could start asking questions again, Melis held out the clothes saying: "Well, get dressed then."

The confused young man was still very surprised about what was happening to him but he took the clothes and quietly got dressed, all the while looking around the cave for answers.

Silem went outside, where he pulled out his Asa Musa stick and used it to summon his flying saucer. He collected all his scientific equipment and took it to his spacecraft before returning and standing at the cave entrance.

As he watched this, Rena/Melis was even more confused and started shaking nervously.

"Now the future is yours, Rena/Melis," said Silem, putting a hand on their patient's shoulder. "I think you will discover many important things for the good of humanity. Before I say goodbye I have one question: when you graduate from high school, what do you hope to do?"

Rena/Melis stopped shaking and thought for a minute before replying: "I will go to medical school. "

"How can you be so sure?"

"When I was a little boy I was ill but it was cured by Turusbek, an herbal doctor. If he was still alive I would be following in his footsteps and would become a great herbal doctor. "

"Do you know what kind of illness it was?"

"Of course, it was cancer!"

"How are you going to find out a way to cure it?"

"I am going to do this using only herbs and natural products. But I am going to do it in a studious and scientific manner with proper experimentation, so I can educate others in the field!"

"Will your life be long enough to do all this?"

"Of course! When I am seventeen, I will start studying at medical school. Afterwards I will work for two years in a hospital, and then I'll have three years of postgraduate study followed by four years of laboratory work. I'll still only be thirty three, and they will be making a golden statue in my village to honour me!"

"How do you know that you are going to do this?"

"I just know. But I can't explain why I know. Maybe some form of intuition!"

Melis, who up till now had been very quiet, took the boy's hand. "Do you want me to help you: shall I study with you too?"

"Yes, of course I really need assistance. I cannot do it all myself. I really need someone of your age who is smart and knows the ways of the world. I need someone who will help me communicate with the Institute of Science, and who would know all about it. Now, could you please introduce yourself, dear uncle: what is your name?

"Melis Uzagalievich Emirov!"

"Stop it uncle! If I am to trust you and we are to share secrets, do not make a fool of me!"

Melis silently pulled his passport from his pocket. Rena/Melis stared at it, then dropped the passport and started shaking. In a trembling voice he asked "Well, who am I then?"

Silem picked the passport up from the ground and gave it back to Melis. He put an arm around each of their shoulders, hugged them both and said "One of you is Melis Emirov, and the other is Rena/Melis Uzagalievich.

"The postman in the village is going to make a joke isn't he, every time he delivers the mail?"

Melis was a little sad.

"Please don't be upset, dear friend," said Silem as he pulled a star-shaped amulet from his chest pocket. "You need this. You will remember me but I may not be coming back again. When I get back to my home planet I will be promoted to the Council Aksakals, and I will forfeit the right to be a spy and to leave the home world.

The ethical laws and the coefficient can't be in equilibrium. I can't hold it anymore. Goodbye, my one heart, there are now three of us".

Silem shook his Asa Musa stick, and was transported to his flying saucer, which in turn vanished into the atmosphere and disappeared.

Melis start walking down and looked in a kindly way at the young man. He was very confused and the realisation of what he had lost, what he had gained and the scale of it all was only now beginning to take shape in his mind, with Silem's departure.

"Renaaaaaaaaaa!"

"Renaaaaaaaaaaaaaa!" He was screaming in his heart. "My precious Rena! I couldn't reach you myself, my dearest love. I will never love again: have I really lost you forever?"

As he struggled with his heartrending emotions, only one song was playing in Melis' ears:

Only sad sounds can I hear
Your playing of the komuz.
We were not always together,
Only my deepest sad story this.
May you dream of many things.
Like neighbours in the next village…

Rena/Melis picked up the framed photograph of Rena. After studying it for a minute or so he felt strange and lonely. He looked around the cave one last time, and then followed Melis out into the new wide world.

Who are we?
One big and open galaxy
The light which brightly shines like morning light

Yes, we are that
We will present clever minds
And move on,
From star to star.

April 1978

THE ROBOT'S BIRTH

Tabyldy was anxiously staring at the screen of the monitor......

He had been working in the Bureau of Designer Construction – a team within The Institute of Applied Science where they made advanced Robots. Robots which could self instruct themselves and were able to develop and have self control to allow them to manipulate themselves in any situation without recourse to instructions. To date the programme had been a success and many of the Robots had developed to very high levels.

However the Robots still exhibited faults. Even when they generated good data from the places to which they had been sent, and these were often wild unearth like environments or extreme highly developed meta-galaxies, if the Developers had not programmed specific instructions then they Robots would "think" very hard about something to the point where it was too much for them. They would frequently get into difficulty and "totally lose their mind" resulting in a loss of functionality and generally reaching a point where they could no longer be of any use.

The Institute were still struggling to explore far, far-away planets of interest due to the limitations exhibited by their Robots.

It was still impossible for humans to fly to far off Galaxies – mankind's' biological life form and life expectancy were too limited. The discovery of travel by the speed of light should have been ten times more powerful in relation to opening up the universe than the previous methods of travel. However the aspects of such fast movement and the unlimited coefficient of time for flying on the human body still - resulted in death straight away for human beings and as such the search for the perfect Robot continued.

The problem of such fast travel for long periods of time had resulted in Mankind turning to the development of fully functioning Robots for space exploration. Many different types of Robots had been made and tested satisfactorily on Earth. However as soon as they were sent to different worlds it was discovered that even the highest developed Robots were still not sufficiently developed in terms of emotional intelligence or senses to make them think through situations. That is why they were still considered to have been failures.

When Robots were "dying" a red coloured button cum buzzer in Mission Control within the Institute would start flashing. This flashing would gradually get more and more regular until the light stayed on permanently and then would get brighter and brighter. The moment of "death" would come when the bright red light would go off.

This time everything was going to plan. Designer Constructor Tabyldy had spent a lot of time carefully creating the Robot he was now monitoring – the Tibald-R000152. It had been sent to the sector of space known as 707*23, planet name A-17 of the star M-00001. Since it had arrived on the planet the Robots had functioned well and the red light on the monitor hadn't even flickered once (which probably meant it had yet to encounter anything strange yet.)

Since he had been jettisoned from planet Earth, Robot Tibald had travelled at an incredible speed over vast distances but had travelled very smoothly with little problems to Planet A-17. It had taken just over a thousand earth days to reach the planet. And since landing he had been consistently sending back messages about his surroundings back to Earth.

The whole design of the Robot was telemetric – a kind of walking TV camera that recorded every movement the Robot made and then transmitted everything back to earth almost like a TV programme.

In his new place Robot Tibald was initially "amazed" to find the inhabitants breathing not with oxygen but some form of jelly. They knew of oxygen but only produced it and admired it as some form of art – as something beautiful and to be admired. Robot Tibalds body had a mechanism known as "X-41" in- built and this allowed his body to adapt after one hour to breathe the jelly atmosphere around him.

After this initial amazement a second startling fact emerged. Instead of eating food the inhabitants listened to music and danced to get their energy.

After a while investigating and monitoring the planet and its inhabitants "Robot-Tibald" knew his food store was finished - he felt that he was getting hungry again.

What to do? He started thinking all sorts of things...

At the same time Tabyldy Designer and all his Institute colleges thought: "That's it, our Robot is going to lose his function as his brain will become completely useless with this very serious question." They were scared!

No!!! Not Yet!!! They were wrong.

Robot Tibald was still "thinking" with a clear and clean mind. Time passed slowly for a long time as they sat and monitored their Robot.

As the Robot became hungrier he began to feel dizzy and his vision became a kaleidoscope of colour. The Robot knew through his programming that as things got tougher that he should be able to come up with some good ideas. And then a good idea arrived in his head.

He added $H2O-12$ with phtor to make a reaction and came up with a thick almost solid like new element –"Space -25" had been invented. This was very edible for the Robot and so he had a very tasty dinner, and loved it very much.

After this episode the contingent of space explorers at the Institute renamed their now great hero as Robot-Robinson-Tibald. They had great expectations that he would now start a new life on his new planet.

Robot-Robinson was deeply impressed with the creativity of the Planets inhabitants and their way of life. All of the population of this planet had great architectural, creativity, painting and art skills which they used to develop something they called the "Whole space cosmological encyclopaedia. " Through this they were searching for the formula of space evolution.

Robot Tibald began to thinking of joining them and helping them in their quest for this "Holy scientific work." After debating for a while he made his first step.

The Planets inhabitants readily accepted the Robot. They thought that the Robot was a prize that they had been given. They thought of him as a unique student of their galaxy for he was always endeavouring to learn. He was rewarded by them with "Pedel" – the highest Government prize. In local terminology it was translated as a "teacher."

Robot Tibald became totally integrated with the locals like a speck of dust within white grain flour. He worked hard at his great space mission.

He was teaching locals items about the "Sun Planetary System" and historical scientific thesis that had been written in the Universities of Earth. This covered everything from biology to physics and also encompassed new and advanced subjects such as Kernel structures and Cosmological roads as well as Earth Art and Literature.

The days and months passed and soon the years began to fly past as well.

On Earth people had started forget about "Robot Tibald-R00007115" and how he had invented his very amazing formula for the wonder food "Space 25."

Robot- Tibald started to feel something as well – the feeling of being bored! Then he had developed the feeling of loneliness and that he was getting old.

These feelings had disappeared however when he saw K-711- a female Robot. Did this mean he was in love? It had happened? Was it impossible?

In the local tradition on the planet a male would pull out his heart and give it to a female to show that he was in love with her. The female would put the heart given by a loved one, into the right side of her body just beside her own. The belief was that this way the lovers could never be separated and would always live together and forever be happy.

Was a Robot capable of doing that? It wasn't in any of his programming or instructions!

Robot Tibald decided it was best to start hiding his feelings and he tried to avoid Robot K-711. The beautiful K-711, one day could pull her heart out and present it to Robot Tibald for on this planet it was all right for females to present their feelings too - they could express their love – as they had equal rights.

What would Robot Tibald do? When Robots were built on Earth the makers hadn't left any extra space for his future wife's' heart! In the local tradition when you don't accept the presented heart it was shameful and the female could even kill the male if he wouldn't accept the presented hearts!

Robot Tibald was hiding from the beauty K-711 although now she was hunting after him; she always wanted to see him. The time had arrived where they had reached the level where they couldn't live without each other anymore.

After many hours and days of thinking things through, Robot Tibald decided that the day had come. Robot K-711 was beautiful as he met her and started walking with her. Even though he felt uncomfortable he didn't mind and in one sweeping movement he opened his front panel and took out his heart and with big respect and pleasure he presented it to his future wife. It looked like it was the right thing to do as the Beauty-K-711, took his heart like it seemed to naturally belong to her and put it in her right side just beside her own.

But at the same time the second body was getting cold – Robot Tibald body was cold.

K-711 looked at her husband and she was scared. Robot Tibald was staring at himself and he could no longer move.

The female K-711 was now holding him and she understood that he was different - he wasn't local, he wasn't a creation of her planet, she now knew his sacrifice for love.

What sadness!

Here, they normally married their own kind. Her new husband and given his heart away to her and was now passing away. He hadn't even tasted the happiness of having a family. What sadness!

When the beauty K-711 realised all this she called the emergency service to save his life. Straight away they arrived and helped keep him alive until they got to an eminent professor. He did some thorough examinations and then with a very serious expression he said:

"Please, do not worry too much. Please, remember you have now got two hearts. We will bring alive your husband in one hundred nineteen- hours!"

At the Institute back on Earth nobody could hear what professor said as the screen had gone blank. The last image that Tabyldy Designer and his colleagues had seen was the six armed and three legged blue- green inhabitants of the planet taking Robot Tibald to an emergency car. The red light had flickered, then stayed on and shone brightly before going out.

Throughout the Bureau of Designer Construction and the whole of the Institute the staffs was sad and the feeling of grief was raw. Tabyldy Designer was crying out loud about the loss of his Robot Tibald.

Then slowly it dawned upon him and he wiped his tears away and he stood up and announced proudly as only he could "Today the Robot is born."

1969

PARADOX

Nurania was a career biologist and this year was celebrating her sixtieth birthday. The celebration had arrived at a good time for her as she had made an important discovery in her laboratory. She had managed to develop a new preparation: a drug that took ten years off the ages of older people. She was immensely proud of her new achievement.

As she looked around the room at her colleagues it suddenly struck her that she had been busy with her career all her life and had never had any time for a private life. Her colleagues were celebrating her sixtieth birthday party as she was always a very happy and a very nice person. However, inside she felt like a child at her eighteenth birthday rather than an old woman.

Her party was going well, and in the end turned into a fine banquet which everyone was really enjoying.

The childish old woman was a little drunk, a little sad and a little lonely. She suddenly looked round, and her eyes fell upon a curly-haired young man. She stared at this handsome male with the strangest feeling in her stomach, and couldn't take her eyes off him.

As Nurania was staring at the young man; she realized that she had never paid attention to a man in this way. This was the first time in her life she had felt such stirrings in her body.

"How damned annoying!" she thought, as she stood amazed at how good-looking this man was. "What hot energy they actually emit when you pay attention to them! They really grab your attention! What wonderful creatures they are! Why did I not know about them until this age? Strange how I never noticed all my friends experiencing this biological wonder when I was a young student! They all got married and had families and children! It looks like men are indeed parts of this very beautiful world are they not? Why should I leave this world unknown and untouched by a man?"

The young man whom the childish old woman Nurania had focussed upon had started his career at the Biology Research Institute two or three months earlier.

"Do you have time for a little private conversation? Perhaps we could go out to talk on the balcony?" Nurania asked with a sly smile.

The young man was called Dias and he was more than a little surprised. For him it was something unheard of to talk face to face with one of the most senior members of the Institute. It was almost like he had been asked to fly seven steps into the sky!

"Pardon... Yes, sure...sure..." he replied stutteringly.

They went out onto the balcony and stood silently together for a couple of minutes, watching the city at night from the seventh floor of the tall building.

Nurania was really shy, and for some reason was struggling to start a conversation. She just didn't know what to say. The young man was very well behaved: with an older person standing with him he knew he shouldn't really start the conversation. He kept silent too.

Time passed. Then Nurania found the courage to speak.

"What do you think, Dias, The world is so wonderful isn't it? So very romantic and poetic, don't you think?"

Nurania was smiling and almost shining in the night.

"I totally agree. The city always looks nice at night," said Dias very politely.

"No, Dias. I didn't mean it in that way. I am trying to say that today is one of the happiest days of my life."

"Of course it is, dear Nurania!"

Dias had no idea where the conversation was heading, but he knew he had to try and be supportive to Nurania. Inside he was thinking "To this old person, the world should be really great everyday!" He realised he wasn't envious of her old age!

"Oh, Dias... Dias... Today is the happiest day I have had. All my life I didn't know about the feelings of love. I fell in love today."

Dias was embarrassed. "Dear colleague, you must be drunk. Please tell this to your friends; friends of the same age."

"I have never been in love with a man in my life! I have never kissed a man in my life! But for some reason today, oh how I would like to kiss a man with my lips! Please Dias, kiss me Dias!" continued Nurania, with her emotions pouring out of her.

"What!" Dias felt as if he had been struck by lightning, and he staggered back and spread himself against the wall. "What did you say, Nurania Naamatovna?"

"Why, you look so pale Dias!" she continued. "Have you never kissed a woman before? Please, can you forgive me? For me, the world without you is nothing. I am in love with you!" Nurania was being very honest with him.

"What?" screamed Dias and he began knocking his head on the wall to see if he was dreaming.

"Nurania Naamatovna, please don't mock me this way. If you would like to sack me just feel free to!"

"Don't talk like a baby, Dias! I was never in love before. I have never loved any man before. I know I have only just met you but I never understood what this feeling of love was all about before. Today I have you, my dear!"

At this, the young man was nearly crying. However he managed to blurt out: "I am only twenty two years old, and you..." His voice trailed off, and then he managed to continue. "Why me? Today is your sixtieth birthday, is it not?"

"Well yes, but why?"

"You are strange! You shouldn't even be dreaming about feelings between us, Nurania Naamatovna!"

"Oh really? No, being in love shouldn't be a problem regardless of age difference! Love is the product of a feeling. There is no set rule for whom you should give it to and whom not to give it to."

"Enough, enough. Enough of this mockery. I can't share your love. Goodbye." And at that Dias turned to leave. Just before he reached the door he turned back and looked at her with very suspicious eyes. "You shouldn't drink unless you know your limit!"

"Is that really true, Dias?" Nurania was very sad.

Dias was a little scared. As he watched her, Nurania Naamatovna started crying, her tears like white pearls rolling down her cheeks. She started talking again in a slightly wicked voice. "If it is only the age difference that is the problem between us and stops us being together, then how old do you want me to be?"

The young man stood silently with his head down.

"Dias," Nurania was crying "Dias, do you want me to be a twenty year old girl? Or maybe eighteen? Tell me?" she was almost begging him now.

"Or maybe even seventeen? I was such a beautiful young girl. What do you think? Are you still single?"

Dias was shaking his head like a drunken man, hearing the words but unable to fully understand what was happening.

"It is true? I really love you? Let's go to my laboratory, there if I drink the new drug I have discovered I will become ten years younger. If I take three further doses that will take me back to the age of twenty again!"

Nurania's sixtieth birthday party was in full swing. People were beginning to wonder what had happened to her. Many people had seen her disappear into her laboratory with Dias, but that had been almost an hour ago. The party had livened up and as the drink flowed everyone was having fun. It was time for speeches, and as the crowd looked around for Nurania, the door to the laboratory opened and Dias walked slowly in.

He was holding a little baby, wrapped up in a white lab coat.

The crowd was totally amazed. He was a single man! Where had he found a little baby?

Dias started talking in a deep and proud voice: "Please meet Nurania Naamatovna who today is celebrating her sixtieth birthday!"

No-one knew what to say.

Eventually Dias managed to tell the story.

In the following days a group of experts picked up on Nurania's research and came up with a press statement:-

"Nurania Naamatovna has returned to a young age through the use of a drug she has developed. She took four doses of the drug. Rather than working four times, this dosage actually produces a cumulative effect some two hundred and forty times higher when taken together. The mistake appears to have been made because our comrade was in emotional turmoil because of falling in love. She probably had not thought through the consequences of combining several dosages. Our sixty year old scientist has turned into a three-month-old baby. This baby girl's condition is very good. She has Normal body temperature and is physically well. She often smiles. She plays and sucks a dummy. The baby is being looked after by a young scientist named Dias, who has taken full responsibility for the child."

All enquiries should be addressed to - The Special Commission of the Biology Institute.

1970

EXPERIMENT

Zakiria was a real practical joker and generally a bit of a prankster. She was always making jokes when she met up with her friends and loved pulling their legs with farfetched stories. She just wasn't a very serious person. Sometimes to make a story or situation really interesting and juicy she would add in made up fantastical "facts" so that her ducks would fly so high. For some reason everything that she made up seemed to be always be believed by everybody.

Sometimes she thought that she would start saying that she was from a different planet and see if they still believed her stories. Yes, she thought, I should experiment with that one.

Zakiria was close to graduating and was extremely busy with her studies and revision and didn't have too much time to catch up with her friends at her College. Tomorrow Zakiria was supposed to go on an expedition with a group of her friends so today she was trying to work on her own.

As she walked down the street she felt very thirsty and she decided to go into her local bistro bar for a quick cool beer. As she went inside she discovered it was extremely busy - lots of other people had had the same idea - and there was a very long queue up to the bar.

Should I stay in such a long queue for one glass of beer? It could take over an hour to get served!

She went straight to the front of the long queue and started talking to the young man who was already at the front. She pretended that she had known him for a long time and smiled sweetly as she asked him to get one more glass of beer for her.

After he had been served the two of them sat down and start drinking their beer. The young man thought "How do I know this girl" and as he looked at her he tried hard to remember.

"We have met somewhere before haven't we?" he enquired.

Zakiria was sipping her beer with big pleasure and as she straight away started teasing the young man.

"Maybe it was on the bus or at the cinema while you were buying tickets or even in the girl's hostel?" she suggested.

Both were laughing. The young man obviously liked Zakiria and they continued the conversation as first one hour then several hours passed by. As the friendship grew and as they finished drinking at the bar the young man offered to walk Zakiria home. As they walked he began to enquire where she originally came from.

Zakiria didn't even think before she replied "From there! From outer space! From the stars!"

"Of course!" the young man laughed at this Joke. He liked such humour. "Which one? And how did you get here?"

Zakiria looked up and pointed to the Planet Mars "Can you see that star there. It is actually our planet. We call it Mars." She had rehearsed her story in her mind several times and now it all poured out. "Yes, we call that Mars too. My grandfather flew to Earth on a research mission and he ended up staying on earth for a while. His flying craft was broken and he could not return. AS he lived here he gradually became more and more like a human. He passed away long time ago but when I was a child he used to tell me lots of good stories about our planet Mars."

The young man looked at her with very strange eyes "Of course! It is always said that anyone who visits Earth from Mars ends up staying here. And of course there were lots of Experimental and Scientific Expeditions. Inside he was thinking "Maybe this creature who talks such lots of shit is actually one of us!" He looked straight at her and asked "Hey, are you telling me the truth?"

"I swear with my life! "Replied Zakiria very seriously.

The Young man started to tickle her feelings and asked "Do you want to visit Mars?"

"Of course I would love to go but it is one of those things – there is just not enough time!" and she laughed "It is very far away and I would get bored on the journey!"

"What if you went with me? I am very good company?"

Zakiria was so glad that he was stringing along the story and was supportive of her jokes. She liked him. Gosh her experiment was working well. "As long as there aren't any more girls I will go with you."

The young man liked her sense of humour and character as well.

"I will swear on my life that I will not tell anyone" she said.

"All right then, let's go." He declared and they walk off down to the fields. The two of them were laughing and joking as they went.

"Oh, what a lovely summers night it is. Walking in the woods; how wonderful it is!" he stated.

So engrossed in their chit chat that Zakiria hadn't even noticed how they had arrived to the middle of the forest. They were both very happy that neither had noticed how far away they had walked.

The young man stopped and said "Well, here is my ship. Let's go in"

Zakiria was very surprised and burst out laughing "Yes of course it is. Where exactly is your space craft?" she said wheeling round with her arms out in what looked like an empty clearing.

At that the young man came forward "Give me your hand, please. Now follow me."
Zakiria was amazed as when she made contact with his hand suddenly she could now see a space ship in front of her. She moved forward and climbed up the steps one at a time until she was inside the space craft.

Zakiria looked around in amazement at the inside of the space ship. On one wall was a monitor – it was truly amazing – it acted like a big eye looking outside into the dark forest. At the other side of from the steps was the main control area with lots of buttons and screens.

As she looked around her gaze fell upon her new friend. She was staring at him – a real man from Mars!

"Zakiria, I don't want to lecture you. I will tell you a short version as you are clever person. I hope you will understand me well. Mars is in the Suns solar system and is one of the most highly developed planets. Mankind believes that there is life apart from that on planet Earth. One of mankind's stated aims is that you should find other such civilisations and develop relationships with them. Is this not true?"

We are so keen to learn from Earth and how it has developed. We have organised scientific expeditions but until now none of the ships have returned back to Mars. I am sure my experience and my knowledge will help me to return back to my planet Mars.

I need however to take back more information and stories about planet Earth. That's why I need some people from planet Earth. It is very important. You already look like a person from Earth. You must come back with me for these two reasons."

Zakiria felt as if she was dreaming and demanded "What! What are you talking about?"

"Dear friend! Don't forget how important the mission is. All of us want to learn and we should share our knowledge as a great experiment about the solar systems planets and let each other know about civilizations of others. If we do not do this it will be a big problem, you must remember that! Your grandfather didn't tell you, about this?

"What, grandfather! I never saw in my life my grandfather or heard something from him about other civilisations. My ancestors - my seven grandfathers are all from planet Earth. Stop making fun of me, no more jokes. I have to go now." Zakiria try to smile."You are really a good joker. It looks like you are also a good illusionist or magic man? Do you work in circus?"

"Zakiria! Please talk seriously!"

"What am I saying wrong?"

"Your grandfather is not from Mars?"

"Of course he is not from Mars – I swear on my life" this time she was very serious with her oath.

"Totally from Earth?" said the young man

"Yes, of course!" extolled Zakiria

"Do Earth people know anything about Mars? That it has life there?"

"Only a little scientific research has been done."

The Man from Mars thought for a while and then made decision "Well, then you have to tell to our scientists about evolution of the planet Earth and how it has developed. If you can tell us everything then my people on Mars will be able to draw information for the benefit of planet Mars.

For you it is going to be a really big plus for the whole solar system and the evolution of civilisation on Earth. To help you must fly to Mars. That will be your new mission!

Zakiria wasn't sure what to do. The Man from Mars appeared very sure of his statements and he sounded so happy.

"Don't be shy. Your cooperation and help for this experiment is Important for both planets and for the future. We should be able to obtain really good results. To be able to develop true and productive experiments for mankind's' future we must be slaves to the scientific mission!

He moved closer to what looked like a control panel and his fingers edged closer to pressing all the push buttons.

Zakiria looked at his fingers, then the buttons and then the large screen that showed the forest outside. It was so dark amongst the trees but as she looked up at the night sky it was full of shining stars. Up in the left quadrant was a brightly shining star – Mars – in all its full glory.

The creatures of the two planets were staring at each other. She let him press the button.

Anyone watching the sky that night would have seen a bright light as the space ship traversed the sky leaving its short signature behind on the big emptiness of space.

1971

SYSTEM THIRTEEN

Marle's father was a very famous designer and a legendary cosmonaut known throughout the solar system and even on the furthest planets. Marles, however, never aspired to his fathers' profession and had had his heart set on becoming a veterinarian doctor. On his 5th birthday his father had given him a state of the art electric radio device but it was of little interest to him and was soon forgotten and lay at the back of his toy cupboard.

When his father had given him this device he was playing with Marles on his knee and he remembered fondly how his father had squeezed his nose so affectionately. He remembered his words as he spoke to both him and his mother "Can you see what I am presenting to my son? This device works even in the thirteenth wave system group. If some day I will have an accident in the space I will send you a signal via this device. From outer space only tis device can accept straightaway signals through the anti magnetic fields and gamma lights. So my son when you get these signals you will know where to search for the signals origin and then you will come and rescue me! By that time you will be one of the best cosmonauts, won't you Marles?"

"No, papa" Marles had said at that time "Instead of flying about space I will go to the mountains catch the tigers, later I could study them... so that I can start my own zoo and help the wild animals breed!"

"Don't say that!" his father had replied laughing at his serious little boy "You will become a cosmonaut. I am sure of that..."

Marles never liked his father's dream. His neighbour at that time – Eridy – had watched his father blast off into space on a spy mission and he had never come back. Eridys' grandmother had waited on her son returning till she was 90-years old. Then she had passed away still crying for her lost son. It had left Marles with fearful thoughts about outer space and a sense of dread in his heart every time his father or one of his friends blasted off even though he understood that every mission was different...

Life could be very similar to other cases...

Marles thought about his father a lot...

He couldn't believe it, how his father could end up like his neighbour – Yrchuul?

Every time when he comes back from school when the Star Union had erected a granite monument in the centre of his town that he had to walk pass every day. The monument had a list of the names of all the cosmonauts on that mission. They had yet to return from space after they had gone to research a star in Vega's Hyperbola. The monument simply said they were lost to space. He used to stare at his fathers' surname. His fathers' image was always with him and he liked to think that he was on his way home after travelling far or that he had been delayed to do something very important and that he was still busy doing this. Marles still felt with his sixth sense that his father was alive.

He had researched the mission and knew his father should have easily reached his destination and that radar contacts had shown this to be the case. The general consensus was that the gravitational pull of Vega was more than first anticipated and that they had been thrown off course as they set out to return to Earth. Radar contact had been lost when his fathers' craft passed behind Saturn. It was thought they had simply got lost in space and with each passing year everyone at the Star Union headquarters feared the worst.

One day, his classmate Ramazan, brought something for him "Marles, please pay attention do not ask me any questions, just listen to me. I have designed a new device which we have to try out to make sure it works. This type of device has already been experimented with but only with limited success. I think I may have solved the underlying problem. You would be a good assistant to me to help me check it out because you are dreaming to go up into the Suusamyr Mountains to do some animal studying. Whilst you are there we can test my device. I know a very nice spot for you that will also test my device to the extreme.

He showed him the map "You should stay at these coordinates and I am going to signal you using the system thirteen."

"Your opening password is "I am Gulistan! Copy West". If I am not responding, press this button to set to automatic and continue your own studying business. My opening password is "I am west! Copy Gullistan." Please check every hour to see if any signal has been received. Now,

I have to go as I have so many things to do and to prepare and I only have this evening. Take care and we will speak tomorrow by system thirteen!"

As he was going away he suddenly turned around and said one more thing "the spot up in the mountains that I am going to is very far away from yours and it will take me a good while to get there. It will take me at least until noon to get there and possibly a good bit longer so you will have plenty of time to go and study the animals. That's why we will only start signalling from 2pm."

As Ramazan left Marles on his own he began to think "Why the Thirteen wave system? Why not the Eleventh or Fourteenth? Why the Thirteenth?" He remembered his earlier childhood when his father had presented him with that device. Maybe Ramazan had remembered and was trying to be clever"

Marles couldn't believe it and started being suspicious. He wondered what the two devices had in common. As it was nagging at his mind he later that day went to his old toy cupboard and there at the back he found his father's gift. He compared the two devices for a long time. Both looked somewhat the same but also different. Both reminded him of a food fixer with a music amplifier and an aerial attached. The one his father had given him looked totally useless and had even started rusting.

He reflected on everything that had happened in his life and particularly how much he missed his father. With a deep sigh he shut away the thoughts and went about preparing for his trip into the mountains and gradually a sense of excitement at seeing his beloved mountain leopards and tigers replaced the thoughts about his missing father.

Marles had arrived at his spot in the mountains after a long hard trek. He was so amazed at the freshness of the wind which was blowing so smoothly. As he looked around the beautiful landscape of the Kyrgyz Mountains was breathtaking. He was now fully focused on trying to observe the wild tiger. As he settled down into his hide he was enjoying his day out.

On this the sunny side of the mountain he knew that the animals would appear to laze in the afternoon sunshine. Already he could hear some baby goat calling on his mother. Farther up circling one of the peaks was an eagle intent on its final approach to its nest. Far away down in the valley he could see day trippers setting up picnics to enjoying the beauty of the day.

At 2pm he set up Ramazans device on a big stone beside him, put on the headphones and then pressed the activation button "I am Gulistan! Copy West!" As he sat and listened all he could hear was an electronic silence with little bursts of unpleasant static coming through the headphone.

Half an hour later... One hour later... One and half hour later ...He repeated the process but nothing. Finally Marles got fed up sitting in the one spot and he had lunch to eat and animals to study! He switched the device to automatic. He was ready for his lunch and as he searched in the bottom of his rucksack for his packed sandwiches he came across the old device which had been given to him by his father.

"Strange, look at me! Why would I bring this one with me as well?" he thought to himself.

After his lunch he tried another time "I am Gulistan! Copy WEST!." Still there was no reply from Razaman.

Marles was curious as to why he had brought his fathers' present. He reached into his rucksack and took it out and attached the spare battery leads from Ramazans device. The little lights flickered and came on. He pressed a few of the buttons and listened to the output but it was the same annoying silence with bursts of unpleasant static that were rapidly giving him a sore head. He put the device beside the other on the rock and lay on his back to watch the blue sky... He thought about his father.

He always thought about his father. Oh, he missed his father so much. Marles wished he could see his father again. He muttered to himself "Father... are you ever going to come back from space?... Ever?..." And at that he closed his eyes and slipped into an afternoon snooze.

The fresh mountain air made him sleep soundly, like a baby. When he awoke it was already evening. "Oh my god! He could hardly believe it. The day was beginning to go and he hadn't really done any studying! "

As he began to find himself he could hear two human voices. As he looked around it gradually dawned on him that they were coming from the devices as if they were talking to each other.

"West, that is understood" said a voice from his fathers' device – the sound of the dynamic assertive voice was shocking and sounded familiar.

"I will report the co-ordinates of "Gulistan." Came the reply from Ramazan.

Marles was confused – who was Ramamzan talking to using his password name of West? Why were the voices so familiar? Was he dreaming? Who was West/Ramazan going to report co-ordinates to?

"West, we have been trying to communicate with Star Union on Earth for years – we do not understand why no-one responds to us. We need help!"

"I do not understand either" replied Ramazan

"West, please confirm that you recorded all our conversation. Are our cosmographia co-ordinates clear? Please go quickly to the Star Union and tell them everything about us. I have one more instruction for you. Please go and find my son Marles and my wife Nargul – they live in Cosmonaut Street, house number 2. If they are still there, then there is electrical device constructed by me, which I gave to my son on his birthday which will work in system thirteen. Please, take that device to the Star Union and then we can definitely communicate directly with the other scientists and work out a rescue plan. Agreed?"

Time stood still - frozen for a second then Ramazans happy voice came over the device "West has your coordinates and yes Comrade, Captain..." Gulistan" your son Marles, my best friend, is still there."

The voice from the device boomed "What? What did you say? You know Marles?"

Marles was sitting and clutching the device and he pressed the activation button and screamed "Faaatheeer! Faaatheeer!"

1968

WITNESS OF THE MIRACLES

On planet Alvendic every street corner, every public square, in front of every large building and throughout every main building there stood some form of sculpture of the young man. They all depicted him with half of his body stretching out through the window of a space-ship with big and meaningful smile and pointing straight to the sun with glorious hope.

The Alvendics are often described with a simple few words - they are the most developed planet in both science and technical art.

When planet Earth was still only in its stone-age period, the Alvendics had already started to send to space ships throughout the galaxy as a very highly developed civilization.

This was the first time that a delegation from Earth had travelled to Alvendic since the two civilizations had met. The occasion was to attend their New Years Ball – all in a spirit of friendship with the Alvendics and other planetary delegates.

The venue for the occasion was in one of the main halls – to say it was large was an understatement. Standing in one corner you couldn't see the other corner. The walls seemed to reach up to the sky and the ceilings were so high it was difficult to even guess how they were supported.

The walls seemed to be made from large pearls that shone and shimmered brightly as if they had captured all the light from the galaxy and of course every so often was another sculpture of the young man in his heroic positions. Looking around it all was mesmerising to the young Earth delegate Nazgul. As she grasped her surroundings she asked her host "Could you please, explain why this young man's sculpture is everywhere?"

"Everyone who is new here asks the same question." Replied Alvina Jiyde, she was their host for the event. "It is a symbol of Remembrance. He was a hero who opened the spaceship era for us. Alas, Genadyi, had a short life. He was only 375 years old when, after he had researched every planet in our galaxy, he went to research the Sun, but he never came back. He was made a hero of Scientific Space for a million years – what we call an Alva- Phansa!"

The guests from planet Earth planet had paid full attention to this story with big pleasure.

"Dear friends" said Nazgul "please could you search from this fine portrayal the determination to explore the Galaxies planets."

She then started to recount her own stories. "Travellers from planet Earth found one planet in the Suns solar system in the North side of the territory of our Galaxy. It was so green and so beautiful. It had similarities to Earth but also to Earths nearest neighbour planet Mars. It had rings orbiting it like planet Saturn and it was amongst these rings that we think we may have found life."

Alvina interrupted "Yes that is correct. In the green orbit life exists. It is a very high civilization there."

"Wow! How do you know that there are any habitants on that planet? Or are you just make it up? You are making a fantasy?" replied Nazgul.

"No. It is not fantasy." Replied Alvina "we communicate with them and have very good and active connections with them. Indeed we have with all life throughout the Galaxy."

Nazgul was amazed "With all of them? Do they all look like us?"

Alvina answered "Yes. As surely as we have contact with you then we do have contact with all of them in the same way."

"It is very amazing." Said Nazgul

"Well now let us all go and watch the performance of eighteen thousand representatives of the Galaxy. Let us see how they are singing songs and dancing and how they are going to enjoy themselves for the upcoming New Year. We can continue this conversation some other time. Please go and meet them all."

Alvina spoke with a very calm voice and was always very polite but she didn't seem to like talking very much.

They all went down to the big hall to watch the New Years Eve performances.

As they began to mingle Alvina introduced various people. It was like a Gallery of Miracles: all of the various people came from different Galaxies and planets and all looked totally amazing and different from one another.

Tense Galaxy's people looked very much like humans – the main difference being that they lived till three hundred years whilst humans only just lived until one hundred years.

Those from planet Gestider had fiery large green eyes and very flexible thin smooth brown body upon which they wore no clothes. Those from Monttors were a bit like humans but pure white.

It was hard not to feel pity for the Abenters who were truly beautiful to look at but only lived to forty one years – that was their life expectancy and their science to date had not improved it at all.

As the Earth delegation moved around to where the Alvendics had a created a beautiful Christmas tree from more glittering pearls they ran straight into other guests they had been trying to meet first: they were from planet Mars.

They were the long headed Martians from the south of the planet. They were having a very serious meeting and talking with great care with some other guests who were representatives of the planet Plutonia. They all met and greeted each other and introduced themselves.

In reality the real miracles were guests from planet Al'ba – this became apparent when it was suggested that everyone should have a little dance with someone from a different part of the Galaxy to help everyone to mix. It should be fun even though the idea of different creatures dancing together may have seemed like a little bit of a silly idea. However as everyone was there to bear witness to the celebration of planet Alvendic there was no excuse and all had to accept the suggestion.

There were very interesting guests. One of them had two eyes on top of their nose and another guest had three eyes up and down his nose. Some of them had three fingers whilst others had as many as twenty. There was indeed lots of different type of creatures gathered here today, for New Year's Eve.

"In my opinion" said Tokon with deep philosophical thoughts "There is no reason to be amazed of these creatures with three fingers and three eyes. Because, it could be simply evolution: somehow parts of their bodies were more useful in some certain times. It is a fine example of the achievements of development and evolution itself. One simple example is that we do sometimes see three eyed fish on the Earth planet. They represent the first step of the evolution although they have survived. You could have an example even some animals: like dogs or monkeys with four legs, and so on and so on. Some of them still have the prints of the two more eyes on above their noses. This may be some useless functions which were unnecessary at some stage. That means that at one time that animal has had four eyes instead, but now it is unrecognizable."

"Maybe, the humans of today used to have four eyes instead of eyebrows. Who knows? We can't say anything for certain we just need to wonder. "

These guests all look from the outside very different but inside they are very much the same as human's like us. They have been using head phones for translating each other planet language so that communications is free and easy with each other and to introduce themselves.

"We are very much well known now to the people from Earth planet."Said Ely from Mars to the other non-earth guests who were surrounding them. She pointed at one of the Earth delegates "This is Nazgul. This girl used to travel to Mars very often. Our relationship with planet Earth is very good. This planet's future is very bright. We do believe that planet Earth could one day invite all of us from all over the various Galaxies to their homeland; it could be soon, in the near future. They are developing very well but still have got some stages to go."

Ely from planet Mars kept on describing to other guests about Earth planet. "It is becoming such a success. We hear lots of good things about planet Earth from others. It makes our people so happy to hear such a good story."

"How old is Earth?" asked a very handsome green eyed young man.

"Seventeen billon years old! And it is only now that it has started to develop." She replied.

"Wow... So Young!"

"Yes, everything is happening at their own pace without any influences from outside." She replied but was stopped from carrying on as suddenly in front of all the tables and chairs for the guest started to grow from the floor.

"These plastic tables and chairs are made from our air." said Alvina. "Nasia is working the controls in our Command Centre. When air is compressed hard it will turn to a liquid and then with help from our technology controls we can turn this liquid fresh air into a plastic that serves us so well. Now with help of some other technology we will soon be served with delicious food."

As he was speaking food materialised instantly on the tables. Alvina proudly gestured them with his hands to help themselves and noted "Here is the era of automatics, technomaticas and bio-electronica for us. It will be a good New Year!!!"

Before entering the big hall, Alvina the hostess of the evening started her speech. She congratulated everyone for New Year, and then she finished her speech.

"Dear, Galaxy people! Do you remember a very long time ago that some planets used to fight with each other? Some of you now do not even know the meaning of the word "WAR". "WAR" is very bad. It was when people killed and destroyed each other. Those days – when people destroyed each other with atomic bombs, which they had made - are completely over and have now disappeared. They have vanished from our Galaxy as we made a law- NO MORE WARS!"

Litts , who was assisting the speaker operated various buttons and a whole Galaxy was portrayed on some kind of monitor on the walls.

"This Galaxy disappeared only one thousand years ago. It was where we learned how to make our plastics from air but now they have disappeared as they could not stop going to war. Do you understand? Humans from planet Earth have developed themselves only by working very hard. They develop Science only for peaceful uses. They are joining with other planets to help promote life. It is a great honour that they are joining our big celebration today."

As Alvina stood a Santa Clause type costume materialised on her and she picked up a little boy and she toasted at the top of her voice "Very Happy NEW YEAR! What a great and happy announcement!"

Everybody nodded their heads with great respect and all were smiling.

Litts, the assistant for the evening raised his glass with champagne as did the rest of the guests as well, and he bellowed "This toast to our future owners of our Galaxy, to Peace and Friendship, and with deep respects for mankind. Let us raise our glasses! Cheers! Cheers every one! To mankind!

1966

HUMAN
OR ANDROID

"Askarbek 2?" said Askarbek while he was getting dressed.

The android, Askarbek 2, didn't look away from the mirror where he was fixing his tie and answered "What do you want to ask? "

It was a very comfortable normal conversation bereft of difficulties. The android was not only an exact copy of him as a man - he was identical to Askarbek. Even his mannerisms and character were almost the same as Askarbeks. That's why in the Cyber-bio-submale Institute, they never really recognized who was the real Askarbek and who was his android copy.

Askarbek continued in a normal business like fashion "What I am going to ask is that today you will take part in the conference I am meant to attend where you will act as me. I am going to go to the theatre and get two tickets because at seven o'clock tonight Laila will return from Ursa Minor to spend her holiday with me. I have to go and meet her as we have promised each other that we will discuss and decide about our marriage."

"OK I See – but ...." replied Askarbek 2 and after a pause continued "...but you should go to the conference and I will meet Laila." As he finished he pulled two theatre tickets from his pocket and announced "I will be going with Laila!"

Askarbek dropped his hat "What!?"

The android calmly bent down and retrieved the hat and as he gave it back to Askarbek he continued "Such is Life. You know I am missing her very much and have been waiting for Laila for such a long time. You of all people should understand me!"

Askarbeks blood was beginning to boil. He stood rooted to the spot and was unable to speak for a couple of seconds before he blurted out "But it is me that is missing her. It is me whose heart has been aching in his chest and longing to see Laila ! What is going on? You are not me! You cannot be missing Laila ! NO! NO!"

Askarbek was very upset but the android didn't seem to notice and kept going almost in a sneering tone "That is not possible today. Maybe I am you! Now just stop ranting"

Askarbek tried to compose himself "I created you as an image of myself: it was me who made you, who gave you life. That means you are mine!"

The android carried on in his conversational tone "Askarbek, I am in a rush, don't make this situation any more difficult than it already is. Of course you have created me. Or is it that I created you. It isn't really clear these days. To be totally honest I think it could be confirmed either way as nowadays nobody can tell us apart. No-one can any longer say who the android is; no-one can tell any difference as to whom the android is – you or me! Both of us have one set of genetics. That's why I am you and you are me. May be you created me but who knows."

Askarbek was dumbfounded "This doesn't make any sense right now."

Askarbek 2 continued on with his logic "To be totally correct it is you who are the member of presidium that means you are going to conference! I have the two tickets and that means I am going take Laila to the Theatre. Well, see you soon, Askarbek!" and at that he headed for the door winking his eye.

Askarbek was boiling with rage. Not sure what to do he stormed after the android as he went outside.

"Oi, oi!!! Askarbek 2! But...But, you, you have never seen Laila in your life. How are you going to recognize her? How? Especially when you have never met her in your life before?" screamed the human Askarbek

"Of course I have." Retorted Askarbek 2

"Then what are you going to say?" asked Aaskarbek

"Don't you remember that rainy night in the train station when I kissed Laila under the bridge?"

Askarbek was so amazed. His veins were bursting, his neck was red. "Damn you, Askarbek!" this time he didn't call the android Askarbek 2 "You have gone too far! How could you? It was me who kissed Laila!"

"Calm down. Askarbek" said Askarbek with a big smile. We are one person, aren't we? I am you and you are me."

The Conference took longer than it should have and Askarbek left very tired. He was slowly walking down the street. He was thinking about Laila. He muttered to himself "Damn! What will Laila and Askarbek be talking about?!" The image in his mind was of his android Askarbek. "Really, is he me or am I him?"

1967